Repentance:
A Tale of Demons in Old Jewish Poland

by

Barak A Bassman

TELEMACHUS PRESS

This book is a work of fiction. Names, characters, places and incidents are either the product of the author's imagination or are used fictitiously. Any resemblance to actual persons, living or dead, or to actual events or locales is entirely coincidental.

Repentance: A Tale of Demons in Old Jewish Poland

Cover designed by Telemachus Press, LLC

Cover art:
Copyright © iStock/23226405_Full_Duncan Walker

Published by Telemachus Press, LLC
http://www.telemachuspress.com

Library of Congress Control Number: 2016943452

ISBN: 978-1-945330-02-5 (eBook)
ISBN: 978-1-945330-03-2 (Paperback)
ISBN: 978-1-945330-04-9 (Hardback)

Version 2016.06.09

Repentance:
A Tale of Demons in Old Jewish Poland

I. The Betrothal

RACHEL PACED BACK and forth in her kitchen. Her eldest daughter, Hannah, offered her a seat at the table nearby, but Rachel's legs had a mind of their own and would not stay still. The only thing that would slow her legs down was the occasional soft chanting sound wafting from the library room, where Rachel's son, Nachman, the town's renowned (if reclusive) Talmudic prodigy was swaying over a holy book.

It was Nachman, in fact, who was the cause of Rachel's nonstop pacing. Nachman had been, for the past year, of marriageable age, and there had been no shortage of matchmakers eager to scoop up the brilliant young scholar for a wealthy would-be father-in-law with a lovely, modest daughter. Given Nachman's prodigious learning and her family's wealth and social standing, Rachel had been sure marrying Nachman off would be a simple task, complicated, if at all, only by the abundance of enticing brides.

But then her husband intervened. Dovid was one of the town's wealthiest merchants, although he had come from a humble background. He had spent lavishly on his beloved Nachman—an army of private tutors and a library of books in the house greater than any in the holy Jewish communities of the Commonwealth of Poland-Lithuania; nothing was too good for Nachman. Yet he dismissed all of the matchmakers without even hearing them out.

What is this madness? Rachel asked him. How do you expect our son to get married if you drive away every matchmaker? Do you think a suitable bride will crawl out of your sacks of grain?

Dovid grinned and shook his head slowly. It was all arranged long ago, he told his wife. Nachman will wed Moshe's daughter. I made this match before he was born, before you and I even met. Sooner or later Moshe will return to town, and we will settle the details. But the match is done.

Rachel was dumbstruck. Moshe was another merchant, from a town far off in White Russia. He was a great hulking giant of a Jew, a veritable Samson (or Goliath) in silk gabardine and fox fur hat. Rachel had known Moshe, distantly, since she was a little girl; he had been a business acquaintance of her father's and was a long-time friend of her husband. Moshe always made Rachel uneasy. She felt he had too much swagger for a decent Jew, and she disapproved of his ability to drink the Ukrainian peasants under the table. There was nothing of the holy, the meek, the pious about him; instead, he was soaked in the carnal pleasures of this world—meat, pastries, vodka, mead, silk clothes, plush carriages. Yet her Dovid was devoted to him.

And it was this Moshe, this vodka-swilling boor, to whom Dovid had sold her Nachman even before he was born. Rachel had raged at her husband that it was madness to make a match for a child who was not yet even born—who would do such a thing? Clearly, she said, such an oath cannot be binding. Just ask the rabbi, she urged, I am sure he will agree.

But Dovid merely sighed, shook his head, and repeated the match was done.

Rachel tried a different tack: Moshe and his daughter are not going to vanish into the fog, she ventured; so until he comes back to town, would it be so terrible to hear what the matchmakers may have to say? No commitments, just listen?

Dovid laughed. The match is done, he said again, and I am not interested in wasting my time.

Rachel groaned and threw her hands in the air. She complained to her friends: My husband has gone crazy. I married an ostrich—he is a great, big, mighty bird that you think would glide through the clouds with outstretched wings, but instead wants to dive his fool head into the dirt.

Yet what could Rachel do? Without her husband's consent no matchmaker could strike a deal. So she resigned herself to wait for Moshe. Maybe, she hoped, Moshe will never come and Dovid will give up these lunatic notions. Or maybe news will arrive that Moshe has made another match for his daughter. Could Moshe really also believe himself bound to this absurd idea of a match struck before the baby's birth? Of course not, Rachel reflected, he has no doubt forgotten this nonsense and news will come of his daughter's marriage to some other groom.

But then one sleepy, sunny afternoon in late summer, a sumptuous wooden carriage pulled by four immense grey horses—angry looking, grim beasts—pulled up in front of the town's inn. The coachman descended from his box and opened the door, revealing a luxurious interior of plush leather seats and wide leg room. Out of the carriage bounded a giant of a Jew, the largest Jew anyone had ever seen, tall as a house and just as broad. Yet his step was nimble and light.

Moshe had arrived in town. The coachman hitched the carriage to a post and watered the horses. After settling on his room and board with the innkeeper, Moshe strode across town to visit his friend, Dovid.

The two of them were now upstairs, almost directly above Rachel and her fidgety legs, speaking to each other about a match between Dovid's Nachman and Moshe's daughter. The two men had been talking for quite some time. Rachel at first had tried to listen in, but to no avail. She was not sure what she wanted: one moment she hoped the match would be struck and she would see her Nachman wed soon, but the next moment she hoped the match would fall apart and she would be free to find a different bride, and a more suitable father-in-law. The sun fell, the moon rose, and still the two men talked together, leaving Rachel and her legs to fret in the kitchen. Hannah eventually sighed, yawned, and kissed her mother goodnight. Rachel hugged her daughter and promised to fill her in on any news the next morning. Rachel thought she should go to sleep, too, but her heart pounded violently and her legs could not stay still. She drank a glass of brandy to steady herself, but it did no good.

Rachel finally heard heavy steps creaking on the staircase. She could hear Moshe and Dovid laughing loudly, and soon the two men arrived in the kitchen with their arms around each other and broad smiles on their faces. Moshe and Dovid sat at the table. Dovid shouted to Nachman to put his books down and join them in the kitchen; he asked Rachel to pour glasses of brandy all around.

Nachman shuffled into the kitchen. He was a wisp of a boy—pale from being indoors all the time, thin as a blade of grass, stooped, and with heavy rings under his eyes. Dovid jumped up from his seat and hugged and kissed his son.

Mazel tov, Nachman! Dovid said. You are to be a groom. Moshe, my great friend here, has a daughter who is a delight—as beautiful as Queen Esther, as pious and modest and loyal as Rabbi Akiva's saintly wife, may her memory be a blessing. Here, grab a glass, let's drink. Let's toast your future, your wedding!

Nachman slowly reached for a glass of brandy. He sniffed the liquor and scrunched his nose. Lifting his eyes to his parents and Moshe, Nachman recited the appropriate blessing and thanks to the Holy One, Blessed be He. Moshe then offered a toast to the new couple, and everyone drank.

Rachel sat down and smiled. She stared at her Nachman and thought how handsome he was now, all grown up, and thought about what cut of suit she would order from the town's finest tailor for the wedding. She knew the scholar had no time for such things.

Dovid laid out the terms of the betrothal. The dowry was large—easily enough to support a man for years—and on top of this Moshe promised free room and board to the couple for seven years, so Nachman could continue his studies without the distraction of earning a living. Rachel smiled even more broadly; she made a silent prayer of gratitude to the Holy One, Blessed be He, for His generosity towards her son.

There was only one condition: Moshe insisted Nachman be taken to meet his daughter before there was a final agreement to the match. Moshe said he would never be accused of trying to sell shoddy goods and insisted Nachman meet and personally approve of the bride. However, as Moshe's villa in White Russia was quite far from Nachman's town, the journey would be arduous. Moshe agreed to take Nachman immediately in his coach, which had room enough for two men (if not more), and to pay all of the boy's expenses. After all, Moshe said, it is not every day a father gets the opportunity to land such a son-in-law. And Nachman will meet and discourse with the finest scholars in each town we pass through.

Moshe leaned back in his chair and looked at the ceiling. He appeared to Rachel to be imagining the bliss of listening to Nachman's imminent debates with sages across Poland and White Russia.

But now, Moshe continued, it is late. I am tired from my travels. Tomorrow I must write a letter to my wife and daughter to share the good news of the match, and then I have a little business to attend to—a man is never free of his business.

Moshe stood, yawned, and waved goodbye. Dovid poured himself another glass of brandy and hummed loudly. Rachel looked at her husband and smiled. Perhaps he was not crazy, she thought. She told herself to trust in him more in the future.

Rachel's peace of mind did not last. The next day she began to worry about her son: Would he be safe on the long journey? What would happen if he should catch a chill? Who would nurse him to health again? Maybe I should go along, Rachel ventured.

Dovid shook his head. Nachman has four younger sisters, he said. You must stay and care for them. I would go too if I could, but I cannot neglect my business for so long. Moshe is my oldest, my most loyal friend. I trust him. He will take good care of our Nachman.

Seeing her son was bound to leave without her, Rachel threw herself into the preparations. The family's best blankets and linens were packed for Nachman's journey, and Nachman was given his father's warmest coat and fur hat. Rachel also fretted about his clothes. He needed practical clothes for the journey, ones that could get soiled and still be worn (after all, who knew when Nachman's clothes would ever be washed properly again). He would also need clothes to honor the *Shabbat*. Most important, what would he wear when meeting his bride to be? Rachel knew she had to make sure Nachman, her prince among men, did not appear to be a *schlemiel*.

Moshe's coachman cursed a blue streak when he saw the bulging trunks he was being asked to haul all the way to White Russia. Didn't this crazy mother realize every inn had plenty of blankets? And the journey would be over before the harsh frosts settled in. But Rachel refused to listen, and Moshe told his coachman to be quiet and to load Nachman's bags.

Moshe walked over to Rachel: Good Mother Rachel, we will take excellent care of Nachman. I have made this journey many times and so has my coachman. Are we sickly or weak? You will see, a few weeks on the road with us, eating what we eat, and your boy will fill out.

Dovid had been staring off into the distance, absent-mindedly twisting the corners of his *tzitzit*, the ritual fringes sticking out from under his shirt, in a steady circular motion. Dovid now suddenly turned to Nachman:

Son, will you write to us? It is a little thing but if you could jot down a few lines at each inn and post them, to reassure us, it would be a great comfort.

Nachman did not hesitate: Of course, at every inn I will post a letter.

The coachman finally succeeded in loading all of the baggage. Moshe practically jumped into the carriage with his long, muscular legs, before reaching down and grabbing Nachman's arms and yanking him up into the enclosed passenger compartment. Moshe pushed Nachman into the seat opposite and handed him a book. Moshe took out a snuff box for himself.

The coachman had meanwhile slammed the passenger door shut and mounted his box. He whipped the horses, and they trotted onto the road. Rachel sighed and felt both sad and proud as she watched her little boy, all grown, go off into the world.

II. Letters from the Road

IT TOOK TWO weeks for Nachman's first letter to arrive. The household had returned to its normal routines. Dovid was busier than ever as the harvests were coming in, and the local lords and their estate managers were negotiating the sale of their excess grain. At home Rachel busied herself consulting matchmakers, discreetly, about Hannah, who was next in line for betrothal. What kind of dowry would be needed? Would the boys find her pretty? Charming? Should she lose a few pounds? Should she have a sample of her sewing ready to be inspected by prospective mothers-in-law?

All this activity distracted the family from their earlier worries about Nachman, until the day Dovid returned home with a short letter from his son, posted from the inn at the town of R____. After the usual greetings and salutations, Nachman informed his father that his journey was progressing well. Nachman and Moshe spent their days in the coach debating the finer points of Torah, and Moshe had turned out to be quite a subtle scholar, identifying tensions and difficulties Nachman had naïvely skipped over. At R____, Nachman had eaten his full at the local inn and spent the day at the town's *Bet Midrash* while Moshe attended to business. He had worked on the problems Moshe had identified in the coach, but could find no solution. Nachman knew the sages of blessed memory could not have engaged in the inconsistencies and errors Moshe had teased out, and therefore, he was determined to find a solution. He knew Moshe was testing him by showing him the difficulties but not their resolution, which Moshe must have long ago discerned for himself. Nachman hoped everyone was well and promised to write again in a few days.

The next letter followed in short order. Nachman wrote that he had solved the problems posed by Moshe only to discover he had barely scratched the surface. Moshe answered Nachman's arguments with more texts showing the sages' comments were contradictory and full or errors. Nachman begged Moshe to clear up these difficulties, but Moshe scolded him claiming that a true scholar would be able to find the answers for himself. So in every town Nachman burrowed deeply into the volumes available in the local *Bet Midrash*. Nachman felt Moshe was the wisest scholar he had ever encountered, and he looked forward to being his son-in-law so they could study together.

It was another month, though, until the next letter trickled in. Rachel had become nervous about the long silence, but she reassured herself that everything would be fine—Moshe was a good man, a fine learned Jew, and Dovid's oldest and dearest friend. Dovid, for his part, told his wife to stay calm and trust Moshe.

Nachman apologized for not writing sooner, but he was engaged in ever more frenzied debates with Moshe. Moshe's sharp arguments had made the words of the Torah seem ever more muddled and confused and absurd. Each time Nachman thought he saw his way clear, Moshe would raise new difficulties sending Nachman whirling into frustration and despair. Nachman had begged Moshe to stop this torment and to reveal the solution to his riddles, but Moshe refused. Nachman was sure Moshe had chosen to test his faith, and to see if he could fight against his doubts and hold firm in the face of such a relentless assault. Nachman was trying his best. He prayed every day to the Holy One, Blessed be He, for strength, and he studied more than ever.

Moshe would go about his business, and he did not disturb Nachman's studies. Yet once they were together again in the carriage, Moshe would again lay siege to Nachman's love of Torah. Nachman would be convinced he had solved the problem and that this time Moshe would embrace him and praise his wisdom. But no, Moshe always had a rejoinder—if not several rejoinders—to Nachman's arguments. Nachman did not understand how a man who seemed never to look into any book, much less a sacred one, could have such easy and perfect command of the holy writings. Nachman felt his years of study had been futile, but he was determined to keep to his faith and show Moshe he would defend the honor of the Torah to his last.

The next letter arrived a week later, but was from Moshe this time. He explained to Dovid that his trip home was delayed by a business opportunity. Moshe wrote he had learned a Polish noble was on the verge of bankruptcy—a combination of gambling debts and demanding mistresses. This noble was desperate to raise cash, leading him to put a tract of land up for sale. Despite an abundance of valuable timber, the price was low because in the middle of the forest on the plot lay a ruined fort, which was said to be haunted by its last defenders, brave Lithuanians cut down by marauding Tatars. The Lithuanians, so the legend went, had pretended to be good Christians, but were secretly adherents of the pagan Lithuanian god, Perkunas, who they claimed ruled the sky and the trees. As their death drew near the Lithuanians had prayed to Perkunas to avenge them. After butchering the garrison, the Tatars feasted on goat meat and drank wine, eventually collapsing into drunken stupors in the fort's courtyard. The Tatars lay down with their puffy drunken faces looking up to the night sky. Then, all at once, simultaneous lightning bolts killed the Tatars at the same time, burning their bodies beyond recognition. Perkunas, the old Lithuanian god of thunder, was said to haunt the fort afterwards, sometimes alone and sometimes with the ghosts of its fallen defenders.

These superstitions had scared off many buyers, but Moshe was convinced it was all nonsense. He and Nachman would journey into the forest to inspect the property. This would be good training for Nachman in the world of business. Nachman was a wonderful boy, Moshe continued, but he had to stop spending all of his waking hours swaying over a Talmud. Moshe planned to teach him how to appraise the timber and to negotiate a land deal.

Rachel shuddered and turned to her Dovid:

What will become of our Nachman? What kind of madman drags a young boy into a forest filled with ghosts and demons? Not to mention sinful Polish lords. Who knows what filthy women that Polish lord has slithering about his palace and sucking his blood. *Nu*, Moshe is a man, experienced in the world, he can take such things in stride. But Nachman, poor Nachman, what will he do? What if some demon has made herself mistress of this lord and she tempts our son? He could lose both this world and the world to come.

Dovid rolled his eyes. Stop worrying, I know Moshe, if there were any real danger, he would not go there. He clearly sees, smart man, that other people's fears—like yours—are creating a golden opportunity. The lord is no doubt a gouty, old drunken fool, and the mistresses are coarse serf girls, not demons, whose like Nachman has seen before. Moshe is a good man, and he has helped me in ways you can never know. Trust him, he is good.

III. Dovid's *Yiches*

DOVID'S CHILDHOOD HAD been difficult. His mother had been a beautiful young woman, tall, haughty, pale, and refined. Her father had been the *arendar* (*i.e.*, the lessee and estate manager) for an absentee Polish noble landlord in Western Ukraine. While the land was peaceful, the *arendar* had thrived: His shrewd, if brutal, management led to surging grain harvests and high profits for himself and his employer living in Krakow. The Ukrainian serfs bristled under the yoke of their absentee Polish lord and his Jewish retainers, and had long fixated in particular on the *arendar's* daughter as the object of their hatred. She was so proud that she would not acknowledge any of the male serfs. The serfs' talk alternated between bawdy jokes at her expense and bitter resentment at her arrogance.

When Chmielnicki rebelled against the Polish crown, his forces swept away the meager Polish Catholic defenses across Ukraine, including in the *arendar's* village. The emboldened serfs burned the synagogue and the *arendar's* villa to the ground. They looted Jewish stores; they chased the Jews away, and beat the stragglers bloody.

But the fate of the *arendar's* daughter was especially bitter. She was the one member of the family in the villa when the attackers came. Before they set the building ablaze she was dragged out from her bedroom and into the courtyard. She was stripped naked in front of a pack of men, who taunted her. The girl stuck to her pride as her last refuge. She closed her eyes and stood stiffly erect and refused to respond to them. The enraged men beat her until she was forced to the ground, where she was repeatedly violated. When it was over she was left lying on the ground, barely conscious and shivering.

The girl somehow pulled herself together, found some clothes, and made her way to the next village, where she reunited with her father and the rest of her family. The household continued to flee, traveling as far from Chmielnicki's hordes as they could.

The family retreated into western Poland, where their lord protected them and gave them shelter on his estate. As they waited out the fighting in the east, the girl began to grow sick. She would vomit each morning, and sometimes in the afternoon as well. She would refuse to eat for days and then eat everything in sight. Her moods swung wildly—happy and carefree one moment, crying and accusatory the next.

The girl's belly grew a bump. She nervously covered it up with loose dresses and aprons and hoped it would somehow go away. She prayed to the Holy One, Blessed be He, to make the bump go away, but it only grew bigger each day. Eventually she could not hide her swollen belly, and she was forced to tell what had happened.

Her father the *arendar* was worried. Not only was his daughter no longer a virgin, but she would now give birth to a *mamzer*, an out of wedlock baby, whose father was some brutally violent gentile serf. What Jewish groom of good family would touch such soiled goods?

Determined his child would live the life she deserved, the *arendar* racked his brains for a solution. He confirmed there were no Jewish witnesses to her shame. Then he swore his wife and daughter to secrecy. He ordered his daughter and one trusted servant to travel to a remote hunting lodge in a pine forest owned by his lord. The girl was left alone in the lodge to give birth in secret. When the time would come, the servant was instructed to find the local Christian midwife and not to reveal the pregnant girl's true identity; the midwife would be told that this was Maria, a Polish servant girl who was bearing the child of another servant who had run away rather than marry her.

In due course a baby boy was born. The *mohel* was summoned for the circumcision ceremony, but the only celebrants were the new mother and the baby's grandparents. The *arendar* named the baby Dovid, after his grandfather of blessed memory. The *arendar* ordered the servant girl to take the baby Dovid to relatives in Galicia. The *arendar* forwarded a letter explaining the baby was an orphan whose parents were murdered by the new Haman, may his name be blotted out, Chmielnicki, in the *arendar*'s former town in Ukraine. The *arendar* claimed his servant had saved the orphaned baby, and he now had to find a home for the child. The *arendar* enclosed a substantial sum to help defray the child-rearing expenses.

The little orphan Dovid was not well-received by his foster family. The *arendar* had chosen them because he knew they would not turn away the extra money, and not because of any great tenderness in that household. In fact, although the *arendar* sent a monthly allowance for Dovid's support, the foster parents never felt it was enough. Making things worse, as the years went by and the *arendar* became confident no one would know of his daughter's shame, he became less punctual in his payments and occasionally forgot them altogether.

Little Dovid, like all little children, was selfish and needy. He would cry at night and demand food, or affection, or to have his bottom cleaned. His foster mother resented her charge but, as a respectable Jewish matron, she could not live with the shame of throwing a small orphan onto the street. So she took her revenge inside the walls of her home.

She refused to give Dovid his favorite foods, even though he could see them in the pantry or the oven. Or she would make him eat only after she had fed her own children first, no matter how much he wailed and cried, and then he could only eat their leftover half-finished meals, which were often caked in a film of his foster siblings' saliva.

This cruelty was not limited to food. Little Dovid's few meager possessions could be ransacked by his foster siblings with impunity, who were also never punished for hitting or teasing little Dovid. When Dovid fought back, however, he was beaten and denied food.

After hearing at the Passover Seder about how Moses had fought Pharaoh with a magic wooden staff that could be turned into a serpent, Dovid decided he wanted a magic staff, too. If his foster brothers or foster mother were mean to him, Dovid would throw his staff to the ground, where it would turn into a giant green serpent with terrible fangs that would force everyone to treat him nicely.

Dovid snuck into the nearby woods to collect various small twigs, which he hid in a fraying satchel. Dovid also stole some string from his foster mother's room. One night, when the moon was especially bright, Dovid used the string to tie the sticks together into a long rickety staff. When Dovid lay down to sleep, he cradled the staff in his arms. It gave him a feeling of safety.

The next morning his foster brothers teased him about his silly looking staff. Moses's staff, they explained, was not patched together from fragile twigs with flimsy lines of string. Dovid insisted his staff was powerful and threw it at one of his older foster brothers. Dovid was sure it would transform into a terrible serpent and eat the wicked, mean boy. It did not; but the hard desperate throw did cut his cheek. Dovid's would-be persecutor ran crying and bleeding to his mother.

His foster mother exploded. She recognized her missing string immediately. Don't you know that costs money, you little *ganef*, you thief, she yelled at him. We take you into our house after your parents are killed, and this is how you repay us? She grabbed the staff. He was denied dinner each night for a week.

The loss of his staff grew in Dovid's mind into a decisive turning point: Without its magical protection, he was helpless. He prayed for a new staff, a staff like Moses's staff, but the Holy One, Blessed be He, did not have time for Dovid's request.

Dovid attended the town's *cheder*, the elementary school, with his foster brothers. He was a poor student—the squiggly letters were always melting into blurs before his eyes and he could never remember exactly how the Biblical passages went—but he cherished the reprieve from his foster mother's cruelty. Dovid would sit in the basement room, where the sun barely shined, even on bright spring days, and lose himself in the comfort of solitude. The teacher rarely paid attention to him as Dovid was, in the teacher's view, a somewhat stupid boy not worth the effort.

After his bar mitzvah Dovid was put to work sweeping the floors and stocking the shelves in his foster father's store. He was not allowed to speak to customers. There were days when he would arrange the inventory in the back of the store and Dovid would lose himself in the peace of solitude. The happiest moments, he found, were the moments when there were no other people around to berate him.

Dovid did not try to imagine a better future; he had trouble imagining any future at all. While his foster parents' children were being betrothed, no one spoke of a match for Dovid. He had no *yiches* (family background, pedigree), no money, and he would never be confused with a halfway literate Jew, much less a scholar. He seemed destined to clean up after others in the store, and to wait out his days in quiet—and deserved—obscurity.

Dovid sometimes pondered the legends of the *lamed-vovniks*, the thirty-six perfectly righteous saints for the sake of whose goodness the Holy One, Blessed be He, permitted the world to exist. The *lamed-vovniks* endured lives similar to Dovid's: poor, abused, scorned, and humble. Yet they were secretly saints possessed of vast magic power and were His favorites; these saints had glorious thrones and palaces awaiting them in the world to come, and would be mighty lords on Earth when the Messiah at last came to redeem Israel from the sufferings of its long exile.

Dovid liked to think of himself as maybe a secret *lamed-vovnik*. He would wait for, and daydream about, the sign from an angel that he was a secret saint. But the sign never came. Dovid would go to bed each night hoping for a dream vision in which the kind angel would explain his true destiny, but his dreams were nothing but a rehash of his foster father yelling at him in the store.

During the day Dovid would also look for signs. Did the dust in the window sill form into letters with a hidden message for Dovid? Or would he find a book mysteriously left open to a page with a hidden message about his destiny? Once more the universe had no message for Dovid, just dust, and curses.

Dovid eventually resigned himself to not being a *lamed-vovnik*. There were far more than thirty-six poor, abused, wretched Jews in the world (there were more than thirty-six in the town) and they could not all be hidden saints.

He had to admit he was also not very saintly. Not that Dovid was a bad Jew—he kept kosher, he prayed each day, and generally observed most of the six hundred and thirteen commandments (although who could fault him for missing one now and again—six hundred and thirteen is a lot to ask of a man with dust in his eyes and a heavy heart). But he felt no special elation when he prayed. The wondrous light of the Holy One, Blessed be He, was not visible to Dovid. He lived in a hum-drum dead end dullness of long, sad, endlessly repeated grey days.

One day when he was sweeping the store, eyes to the ground as always, Dovid overheard two men talking: They had both heard it finally had happened—the Messiah had come. It was time to sell everything and to leave Poland for the Holy Land. There would be no more suffering or disease or poverty. The bitter exile was ending and soon every Jew would live like a lord, with milk and honey and orange groves.

Soon everywhere he went Dovid heard about this newly-arrived Messiah. His foster parents were skeptical at first, but even they became carried away. Soon they, too, were planning their journey to Jerusalem.

There were ecstatic celebrations. The Messiah, who resided in the Kingdom of the Sultan of the Turks, had announced there was no longer any need for the prohibitions of the law. The commandments had existed to enable the Jewish people to raise the sparks of holiness scattered at creation when the Holy One, Blessed be He, compressed his being to make room for the world. Now that the sparks had been found and redeemed and the Messianic Age had arrived, there was no longer a need for the Torah's prohibitions. What was forbidden was now permitted, if not affirmatively commanded.

Jews went out of their way to show allegiance to the new Messiah through a deliberate breaking of the commandments. Gangs of men would light their pipes on *Shabbat*. There were gatherings in town where *treyf* food was served and women danced naked, shamelessly, in front of the assembled men. The Jews gloried in what was once forbidden, but was now permitted, if not commanded, by the newly revealed Messiah.

Dovid was hardly a leader in the Messianic movement; in truth, he barely participated. He had overheated dreams of dancing naked women, but never learned where these gatherings were, much less attended them. He tried to eat a piece of *treyf*—a slice of ham left in the store by an ardent disciple of the Messiah—but the smell nauseated him. Nor could Dovid make plans for a trip to Palestine. He had almost no possessions to sell to raise money for the journey; he would have to wait for an enchanted cloud to pick him up amidst crowds of other Jews and transport him to Jerusalem.

Still, the advent of the Messiah gave Dovid a particular hope. When the Messiah raised the dead, he would bring to life Dovid's parents, whom Dovid had been told were righteous Jews murdered by Chmielnicki and martyred for *Kiddush Hashem*, the sanctification of the Holy Name. His real parents would kiss and embrace him. In the Messiah's Jerusalem Dovid would live with his parents by an orange grove and smell the cool air at dusk. His parents would find a resurrected girl, maybe another martyr from their village, for Dovid to marry. He would live for eternity in love and comfort in the Holy Land and could forget his cruel foster family. He was sure they would be punished by being sent to live in an unfashionable part of the Holy Land, probably some desert far away from the orange trees where the milk would be sour.

And then everything changed. The Messiah, Sabbatai Zevi, was captured by the Sultan. The Sultan gave the Messiah a choice: death or conversion to Islam. The Messiah did not use his great powers to overwhelm the arrogance of the gentile monarch. Instead, he became a Muslim.

The Messiah's wild adherents became rabid penitents. Rabbis across Poland excoriated their flock for embracing the false Messiah and heeding his cries to abandon the commandments of the Torah. Fasts abounded, and everyone scrambled to be more pious than ever.

The once again pious Jews turned on the Messiah's remaining obstinate followers. Those followers tried to justify his actions: The world was not ready for redemption, it had to be made more sinful before the Holy One would redeem it; the Messiah had nobly dived ever more deeply into the world of falseness and depravity so that he could usher in the Messianic redemption. But the bulk of the community would have none of it; the false Messiah had been exposed, and his lies had to be stamped out. Sabbateans either fell into line (publicly, at least) or were forced out.

Dovid was hit hard by the fall of the false Messiah. He had felt not Israel's imminent redemption, but his own—his true, loving family resurrected from the dead and a new home in the Holy Land. Now he was told it had all been lies, and the world he had known— of sweeping dust and bearing petty cruelty—was the true world.

Dovid was cleaning in a corner of his foster father's store when he overheard a group of Jews mocking the false Messiah, Sabbatai Zevi, and gossiping as to who may still be foolish enough to follow the apostate fraud. They laughed at the silly notion that the Messiah would cower before an earthly king like the Turkish Sultan.

Dovid felt his anger rising. He saw his imagined dead parents standing there, modest, poor folk who had been hoping to be resurrected from their graves so they could find their long lost orphan son. Dovid saw his imagined ghost mother in a tattered dress, with a woolen shawl and a kerchief wrapped around her head; his father had a scraggly beard and wore a greasy, stained gabardine. Each time the living Jews laughed, the ghosts looked at the floor and shed quiet tears. Dovid was furious at these Jews for mocking his poor parents, and he felt guilty as he watched the ghosts meekly suffer such abuse at the hands of the town's arrogant rich.

Dovid could stand the cruel jests no longer. He threw his broom at the group of chattering women, hitting one of them in the leg. The women fell immediately silent and looked over at Dovid. He looked back with wild, feverish eyes. He stared and breathed hard; his fists clenched. Dovid spoke in a loud voice he did not know he had:

He was not a false Messiah. He was sent by the Holy One, Blessed be He, to redeem us, and he will raise the dead. The dead will be resurrected soon, in our lifetime, and they will scold you for your cruel words. You are laughing at our dead, may their memories be a blessing.

The women quickly left the store. Dovid's foster father returned from the back to find the store emptied, the broom lying on the ground far from Dovid, and Dovid shaking violently. Outside the window a group had gathered, whispering and pointing to the store.

What is this, Dovid? What has happened? Where are the customers?

Dovid said nothing. He looked down. His foster father walked up closely to him, leaned his mouth to Dovid's left ear, and repeated his questions with a sharp shout. Dovid shoved him away and walked out through the rear of the store.

Dovid walked into the nearby forest to a sweetly murmuring spring where he sat and cried. He did not want to leave the forest. Dovid drank from the spring, put his head on a stone, and felt himself sink into a comfortable bed of dirty moss. He prayed to the Holy One, Blessed be He, to reveal the Messiah's true identity. And he prayed that the apostasy was merely a clever test of Israel's faith—and that he, Dovid, was one of the wise and pious who had passed this cruel, difficult test.

Dovid lost track of time. It was dark except for the moonbeams flickering weakly between the thick foliage overhead, and his stomach twisted in pain from hunger. Dovid rose slowly; he felt sharp pain in his sore neck and back. In the feeble moonlight he could see no fruit to pick, so reluctantly and slowly, he trudged back through the forest path, into town, and to his foster family's home.

Dovid pushed the door open and walked in. Facing him, in the yellow candlelight, was a room packed with indignant bearded faces, many grey and wrinkled. The town's richest man and chief officeholder, the *parnas*, approached, with the rabbi in tow.

The *parnas* spoke:

Young man, we have been told that you have proselytized in the cause of the false Messiah, Sabbatai Zevi, may his name be cursed and forgotten. Is this true?

He is not the false Messiah. He will raise the dead soon. The Holy One, Blessed be He, is testing us.

The *parnas* hit Dovid with the head of his cane, knocking him down, and continued speaking:

You insolent fool. The Messiah does not abandon his people and convert to another faith. You have always been a good boy, eh? Who put this nonsense into your head? Tell me the name and we can let you be. A deceiver has seduced you with lies. Tell us who the real heretic is, so we may cleanse our holy community.

Dovid wiped the blood from his fresh wound onto his sleeve and pulled himself up by holding onto a nearby chair. Dovid looked up at the *parnas*. He was calm.

No one whispered anything to me. The Holy One, Blessed be He, gave me a vision of the dead resurrected.

The *parnas* straightened his back. He hit Dovid again with his cane, sending Dovid staggering back to the floor.

If you continue with this heresy, you will have to leave our town. Think over tonight what you have said, and what is true and what is false.

The *parnas* left with the rabbi and the other men trailing after him. Dovid again pulled himself up. His foster parents and siblings stared at him with a mix of bafflement and terror. Dovid grabbed a half-eaten loaf of black bread from the table and scampered up to the small, damp attic where he slept on a pile of straw.

Dovid was awoken the next morning by loud banging on the door to the attic. He rubbed his eyes and saw the sun was high in the sky. He had overslept; he was late to the store. He dressed quickly, and hurried down.

Dovid was greeted by his foster father and one of the town's wealthy citizens, a brother-in-law of the *parnas*. Dovid was given an opportunity to repent his heresy—a last opportunity, as was made quite clear.

Dovid sat on a chair and looked at the floor. He knew he should repent. He had never been involved in the Messiah's movement, he had merely watched—or, more precisely, heard—events from the distance of his lonely, solitary corners in the store. Dovid was not even entirely sure what the false Messiah actually preached.

Just say the words—I repent, I am sorry—and be done with this all, Dovid thought. He wanted to speak these words, but then he saw them again, the ghosts of his imaginary parents. Shivering in their tattered clothes, they said nothing, but their expressions pled for mercy. Dovid felt to deny the Messiah was to hurl these two, who loved him so dearly, back into their graves to be eaten by worms and tormented by laughing demon imps. He could not betray them.

So Dovid made his fateful decision:

Sabbatai Zevi is the true Messiah, he said, and he will raise the dead soon, very soon. We will all join him in Jerusalem.

Dovid was instructed to pack his belongings and to leave town. His few clothes, his *tfillin* and prayer shawl, and a book of psalms, all fit into a small, weather beaten satchel. Without any lingering goodbyes, Dovid walked out of town on the main road.

IV. Dovid and Moshe

AFTER STEALING FRUIT from an orchard, Dovid walked two days under the hot sun until he reached the next town, arriving tired and hungry. He was sent to stay with the other beggars in the poorhouse next to the synagogue, where he was fed scraps of bread and cups of sour wine by the synagogue beadle.

The poorhouse was dark, and stank of sweat and urine. The men packed inside—for they were all men, the beggars in this particular poorhouse—were a gruesome spectacle: many were missing at least one limb, one had his nose and lips cut off, another had lost an eye, and left his empty socket exposed to the world, and yet another man had strange boils covering his body, which he picked at, leading every now and then to an eruption of sticky white puss.

The men's talk was a good education for a novice beggar such as Dovid. They swapped information as to which towns had the best poorhouses and begging opportunities, compared their pleas, and critiqued one another's presentation. Each beggar claimed to be a victim of Chmielnicki's men, maimed and brutalized for refusing to be baptized. Sometimes the men claimed to have starving orphans back home. They interrogated each other closely as to whether one variation or another of their tales elicited more sympathy.

Dovid had slinked off to a corner where he could sit directly under a lamp. He was quietly reading his book of psalms, although he barely understood any of the words and knew he was mispronouncing the Hebrew. The one-eyed man prodded Dovid:

So what is your story? You don't look like a sad enough case. You have a book? Do you tell them you are pious? Collecting money for the Jews of the Holy Land? Selling magic dirt from the Holy Land? I did that once. Although the dirt was from the banks of the Dnieper.

The beggars laughed.

Dovid concentrated on his psalms while cursing himself for being such a poor, slow reader. He told himself he was praying for his parents, whose souls savored his words, broken and jumbled as they may be.

Speak up, boy. You are being rude to your distinguished elders.

More laughter.

I was told to leave my town. I stayed true to the Messiah, Sabbatai Zevi.

The one-eyed man frowned:

The Messiah story does not work anymore. No one wants to hear it. And you better stop talking about it here. If that beadle hears your Messiah talk, he may decide we are all no good heretics and there will be no more coins and no more bread. Do you understand?

The one-eyed man had grabbed a stick and was holding it tightly. Dovid said he understood and just wished to pray quietly.

The other beggars resumed speaking to one another and ignored Dovid once again. Dovid's eyes became heavy with sleep, and he drifted off sitting upright in the corner and holding his book of psalms to his chest.

When he woke in the morning Dovid found himself alone in the poorhouse. The other beggars had gone and they had plundered his meager belongings, save the book of psalms he still held in his hands. With nothing else to do, and no one to turn to, Dovid stretched his limbs and continued to chant the psalms. Maybe he would get better with some practice, he thought.

When the beadle returned, he asked why Dovid had not traveled to the wedding with the other beggars.

What wedding?

Next town over, a rich man is marrying off his only daughter and had promised to feed all the beggars lavishly. I thought that was why you came here. Like the others. But it is probably too late for you to get there now.

The beadle paused. He looked at Dovid, and saw the book in his hands.

What are you reading?

Dovid showed him the book.

You can read psalms?

Yes. Not as well as I should, but yes.

The beadle grinned.

Good, I could use a psalm reader. When I receive money for psalms to be read for the sick or the dead, you will stay up day and night reading them. I will let you sleep in the synagogue attic, and away from the beggars. You can eat *challah* and drink wine, maybe some carp or goose now and then. Agreed?

So Dovid settled into his vocation as a psalm reader. Whenever a Jew in town died, Dovid was summoned to stay up all night with the body and to read psalms to protect the soul of the dead person from assault by demons and other evil spirits. He was often treated to cakes, cookies, meat, and wine by the family in gratitude for his services. Slowly, through these nocturnal visitations, Dovid became known to the town's Jews, who viewed him as upstanding and pious, but also shy and simple-minded.

Dovid also was assigned to read psalms for the sick when an ill person's family paid the beadle for a lengthy session of psalm reading in the synagogue. The beadle would fetch Dovid, who would sway back and forth reciting psalms without stop until the beadle told him there was no longer any need.

When he was finished, Dovid would trudge up to his attic room and collapse from exhaustion. He sometimes slept twelve or fourteen hours after these long prayer vigils. He was lucky when he was able to get all of this sleep, though; sometimes the beadle would prod him awake with his staff, a quick stab to the ribcage, as the sick or dead were again in need of psalms.

Dovid at first practiced his psalms during each spare moment. He was terrified he would make a mistake, be uncovered as a fraud, and lose his newfound livelihood. Yet within a few weeks Dovid discovered he had thoroughly memorized his slim book of psalms. He had so mastered his material he often answered questions from the townspeople with quotations from psalms.

Dovid's conversations, however, were few and far between. He recalled well how a loose tongue and excessive candor had led to his expulsion from his childhood home. Determined to avoid the same fate, Dovid stayed quiet. He declined to discuss his background or family, and only said cryptically he was a humble stranger who trusted to the generosity and friendship of his fellow Jews.

To avoid uncomfortable conversations Dovid spent his free time walking in the nearby forests, enjoying the smell of the damp leaves and the sounds of the birds. On these walks he would dream of the Messiah's coming, the resurrection of the dead, and his reunion with his parents.

A couple of years passed in this manner. Dovid ceased to be a curiosity to the town's Jews and faded into the background of their community. His familiar, quiet presence was reassuring to the grieving, and he was viewed as the town's holy fool.

Every so often the question would arise as to whether Dovid should marry. Obviously the town's wealthy Jews had no interest in such a groom. While the poor families admired him they worried how Dovid could support a family when his only trade was reading psalms. So Dovid lingered as a bachelor, which was fine by him: He lived in the dream world of an imaginary restored Jewish kingdom in Jerusalem, ruled by the Messiah, where he and his resurrected parents tended their orange grove together. Once he was established in the Holy Land, Dovid mused, he was confident a friendly angel would introduce him to his *bashert*, the bride destined for him by heavenly decree. Until then, he could wait and enjoy the solitude of the forest and the occasional treat of goose fat spread on fresh warm bread.

Dovid's dreamy idyll ended with the death of a wealthy merchant. This merchant had leased the local distillery and inn from the town's Polish lord and turned a huge profit selling vodka in the region, although the merchant was also rumored to partake too readily in his own wares and to be too familiar with the Ukrainian serving girls in his employ. Nevertheless, the grieving family summoned Dovid to attend the dead body for the night before the burial and to recite psalms for the man's somewhat tarnished soul. Dovid took up his perch at twilight and swayed and prayed all night over the corpse. The widow was kind enough to send her servant in with butter cookies and warm cider.

As the sun rose and brightened the room with a pinkish light, Dovid felt weariness creep into his bones. He expected the burial society to arrive soon to prepare the body, which was his signal to leave for the synagogue attic bed. However, this time, before the burial society came, a tall man with broad shoulders entered. Although clearly a Jew, he was far bigger than any Jew Dovid had ever seen.

The hulking Jewish giant was elegant in his dress and bearing: He wore a silk gabardine and shiny leather boots; his shirt was snow white and freshly starched, and his pants were unwrinkled. The man sported a long, thick but neat and well-tended black beard.

The Jewish giant sat on a chair near the dead body and watched Dovid as he swayed and recited the psalms. The man did not move or speak. His stare made Dovid uncomfortable, but Dovid reminded himself this was probably a relation of the deceased who was still in shock and trying to find the words—or the heart—to mourn.

In due course, the men from the burial society came. Of course, Dovid and these men knew each other quite well by this time. Upon their entrance Dovid stopped his recitation, closed his book, and stepped away. The chief of the burial society thanked Dovid for his tireless prayers and gave him a couple of coins. Dovid mumbled his thanks back along with a couple of appropriate quotations from the psalms. Dovid left the room where the body lay, walked into the foyer with his head bowed down, and then slipped out the door. The harsh morning sunlight stung his tired eyes. After these exhausting all night vigils, Dovid always felt lightheaded and slightly unsure of the boundary line between the real waking world and the world of dreams.

However, a few minutes later, as he stumbled back towards the synagogue and his attic bed, Dovid felt a huge hand fall on his shoulder. Dovid stopped and turned, and saw the same Jewish giant.

Please sir, come with me to my inn. I will buy you breakfast. You were so good as to pray for the soul of my dear friend, I want to do something to show my gratitude before I leave for the funeral.

Dovid felt too tired to resist and, anyway, who was he to turn down the offer of a good meal? So Dovid followed the giant to his inn.

Over breakfast Dovid learned this new Goliath was named Moshe, and he was a wealthy merchant from a distant town in White Russia. Moshe had enjoyed lucrative business ties with the deceased and had arrived the previous night to conduct a little bit of business and a little bit of drinking, only to discover his friend had died suddenly. Unable to sleep, he had decided to go to the body to ensure psalms were being said for the dead man's soul. And there he had found Dovid.

Then Moshe said something that surprised Dovid, although he put little weight upon it at the time. Moshe stated the problem for the dead was not harassing demons, whom he insisted were a decent, honest lot with their hands full running *Gehenna*, Hell, as well as performing the occasional tiresome errand on Earth. Rather, it was those avenging angels with their fiery swords, judgmental know-it-alls who smugly pronounced their own sentence before the soul could reach the Heavenly Tribunal for trial. They were the ones who tormented the souls of the dead and tortured them prematurely. Moshe smiled and said the psalms protected the dead from angels, not demons.

Moshe asked Dovid about his background. Dovid demurred and quoted his psalms.

What do you want out of life? Moshe asked. You cannot expect to live out your days as a bachelor mumbling psalms day and night. Surely you must want something? You are a young man, with a young man's needs—don't you desire a wife?

Dovid blushed. He replied softly he only wished to submit to the will of the Holy One, Blessed be He, and if it was his fate to live out his years as a poor bachelor, then so be it.

How can you already be so defeated? *Nu*, you are not an old man yet. What is this craziness? You have spent too much time with the dead. Look at that girl, by the bar, the young Polish girl with the big, healthy chest—she doesn't make you want to be a husband?

Dovid blushed more deeply and did not speak any further. Moshe slouched back and drank more tea. After a pause, he told Dovid to return to his room and to get some sleep. Moshe promised to think up a solution for the young man's predicament. This was no way to live. Dovid thanked him for breakfast and went home, where he collapsed into a black sleep for the next several hours.

Dovid awoke at dusk. He stretched his limbs, yawned, and walked downstairs for his evening prayers. He found his usual seat in an alcove in the far west of the sanctuary, away from the town's notables on the eastern wall, and prayed quietly.

Moshe walked over to him. Moshe had not been praying, but was instead speaking, and not quietly, to various business acquaintances. They laughed and joked, and ignored the dirty looks of the more pious worshippers.

Moshe clapped Dovid on the shoulder. Come with me to my inn again, he said, let us share a drink. I have thought about your problem and I have a solution. You may find it unusual, but I think you will realize it is for the best. Come, let's go. The synagogue will wait for you to come back and say more prayers later. I am sure these walls are tired of the sound of melancholy Jewish men weeping to Heaven. For the sake of the suffering walls, come with me.

Dovid looked at his feet. No, I can't, you have been so kind and generous already, Reb Moshe, I can't impose further upon you …

Nonsense. Come. Come now.

Dovid found himself walking in the chilly night air. He and Moshe seemed to float to the tavern where Moshe had a table waiting and where he promptly ordered two glasses of vodka. Moshe spoke to the waitress in what Dovid felt was a too familiar tone.

There was a rowdy party of serfs at the next table, drunk and singing, who leered at the waitress and whistled and offered to take her home. At first she smiled and laughed and teased them back, but when they did not relent, her smile faded. The waitress backed away behind the tavern counter and asked the old innkeeper's wife to serve them in her stead. The men stopped laughing and demanded their original waitress. Their voices rose. A bottle broke; a fist slammed. The group rose together and staggered forward.

The innkeeper entered the tavern area, holding a club and flanked by his two sons also carrying clubs. The innkeeper told the drunken serfs to leave. He reminded them they had work to do the next day and wives at home. The men—who were no longer young, even if not quite old yet—relaxed their muscles, hung their heads, and walked out. The waitress stayed behind the counter and did not look at them.

Moshe watched this scene unfold with a smirk. He was clearly amused and, at the end, caught the waitress's eye and winked at her. She turned her head away. Moshe laughed softly under his breath and took another drink of vodka.

Dovid had taken two or three quick, clumsy gulps from his glass, which was still more than half full. He was lightheaded nonetheless, as he was unaccustomed to the strong liquor. His throat and stomach burned, and everything seemed too loud and too fast. Dovid was uncomfortable with Moshe's glee at the drunks' aggression towards the waitress, and he started, slowly, to try to stand up.

Moshe grabbed Dovid by the shoulders and pushed him back down; Dovid acquiesced. Moshe leaned so close to Dovid that the two men could feel each other's breath and now whispered his proposed solution to Dovid's problems:

I see you are losing patience. Your soul is not used to such coarse surroundings. You are so accustomed to the holy aura of the dead you can no longer bear the rotting stink of living souls. No more dawdling, I will get to the point. I have many friends among the rich in this town, including the old grain merchant, Yosl. Yosl has one unmarried daughter, the surprise child of his old age, lovely young Rachel. If you want, I can arrange for you to work for Yosl. You can help with his accounts, learn his business. You can board in his home—Heaven knows he has the extra room these days. Give Yosl a little time and he will want to marry you to his Rachel. You can be a wealthy householder, inherit the business, and have a litter of children. How does that sound, eh?

Dovid burst out laughing.

You don't believe me, do you? Don't be so skeptical. There are greater powers in the universe and perhaps they have plans for you. I can make this happen for you, but I need something in return from you. Are you interested?

Dovid shrugged. Why not? What is your price for a miracle?

My price is simple. Your firstborn son will be married to a daughter of mine. And I do not want just any boy whom you might raise however you see fit. No, this boy must be brought up to my—how should I put it—to my specifications. He must be drilled day and night in Torah, in Talmud, in the commentaries. He must be pushed—forced—to be a scholar. You will nurture a son-in-law for me to my specifications, and in return, you will be a wealthy man. Do we have an agreement?

Dovid looked at Moshe as if he were crazy. At the same time, he thought, why not? Moshe means well, although he must be drunk. It can't hurt to play along with this game. What could happen? So Dovid agreed.

Wonderful! *Mazel tov*! Moshe shouted. To your coming years of happiness and wealth!

And Moshe drained his glass of vodka, grabbed Dovid's still rather full glass, and then drained it too. He clapped Dovid on the shoulder and stood up. Help me back to my room.

Dovid stood up and let the inebriated Moshe rest his weight against him. The two waddled behind the tavern area to where Moshe had his room. Moshe kicked the door open and fell down upon the bed. Dovid helped to remove his boots.

As Moshe was drifting off to sleep, he told Dovid:

You made a wise choice tonight. Great blessings will soon come your way. I am a man of my word, and I expect you to keep your promise to me, too.

The words trailed off, and Moshe's eyes shut and his breathing slowed. His powerful, satisfied snoring filled the room and echoed against the walls. Dovid quietly left and closed the door behind him.

Once Dovid left the inn he was enveloped by the silent icy night. He reflected that the sober people of the town had long since gone to sleep. Dovid was grateful for the sharpness of the chilly night breeze, which smacked him out of his warm drunk haze. He walked back to the synagogue, climbed into the attic, and fell asleep.

Dovid thought little of Moshe's extravagant promises, especially after learning the next morning that Moshe had left town. He assumed Moshe was a lonely drunk who had latched on to him and his grand oaths might as well have been written with wind and water.

Nevertheless, something curious happened roughly three weeks after Moshe left town. Dovid was awoken in the middle of the morning by a loud bang upon the door to the attic.

Dovid, get up, come downstairs. You have a visitor, an important man. Hurry up.

It was the beadle. Dovid could not imagine what this could be about, but pulled his clothes on and stumbled downstairs. His limbs felt heavy and the light was painful.

Next to the beadle was Yosl the grain merchant, a small man, old and bent, with a wisp of a grey beard. The beadle told Dovid that Yosl wanted a word with him in private, and then left the two men alone. Yosl motioned to walk with him to his seat by the eastern wall of the synagogue.

Yosl held Dovid's hands in his own, and spoke softly:

Dovid, my son, Moshe told me the truth of your ancestry. That you are the child of the daughter of a distinguished *arendar*, one of the most distinguished Jews in Ukraine before Chmielnicki's massacres. He told me how you wound up with uncaring distant relatives, but said you have wondrous gifts that show your true, fine lineage. Moshe begged me to take you into my employ, so you could learn about business and your natural talents could get a chance to shine. I agreed, and I am here to fulfill my promise. Will you come to work for me? I am sure my wages will be better than whatever the beadle gives you to murmur psalms over corpses.

Dovid could not believe his ears. Ignorant of his true family history, he was sure Moshe had lied to Yosl and made up this absurd story about his supposed illustrious ancestry. Dovid felt he knew who his real parents were: the two humble souls whom he had seen in his visions when the Messiah's advent had seemed so close. Dovid had no intention of playing along with Moshe's ridiculous deceit.

Reb Yosl, you are too kind. I have no such fine ancestry. I am a poor man, with little learning, from a poor home. I have no trade and no knowledge of business. I am a hopeless fool in the world. I know nothing but the beautiful psalms, and I only want to serve and glorify the Holy One, Blessed be He, as best I can in my own small way. I am afraid I would be of no help to you, but would only be a burden.

Nonsense. Moshe told me you were humble and determined to cover up your illustrious family in order to pretend to be some kind of *lamed-vovnik*, a hidden saint. Well, you have suffered enough. You do not have to disdain this world to gain the world to come. The Rambam was the wealthy physician to the King of Egypt, and Rashi owned vineyards in France. If these great sages could attain their rewards in both our world and the world to come, who are you to refute them? As for being a burden, it is my business and my money. I will be the judge of who is and who isn't a burden to me.

But where will I live? If I leave the beadle, he will not let me sleep in the synagogue attic.

I have extra space in my home. My wife, may her memory be a blessing, passed away many years ago. My children have all moved out save my Rachel, the child of my old age. She is my comfort. I keep telling her I need to find her a husband, but she will hear none of it. She wants to take care of me, she says. What can I do? It will be good to have someone else around the house. Consider room and board to be part of your wages.

Dovid could not believe what he was hearing. He had tried to set the old man straight about Moshe's lies. Even now, though, having heard the truth, Reb Yosl still wanted to go ahead with his plan. So why not agree? Who was Dovid to turn away a warmer bed, better and bigger meals, and maybe even some money in his pocket? Who was to say this was not his reward for all his good deeds? Perhaps King David, in Paradise, had heard his earthly namesake's devotion to his beautiful psalms and beseeched the Heavenly Tribunal for a kind decree to ease Dovid's suffering?

So Dovid agreed to work for Reb Yosl and to board with him. Yosl clapped his hands in delight and ran off to find the beadle. When Yosl returned he told Dovid to pack his belongings. Dovid dutifully returned to his room in the synagogue attic, packed his few possessions into a small satchel, and came back down in less than a quarter of an hour.

Where are the rest of your things? Yosl asked.

These are all of them.

Yosl sighed. Yours has been a cruel fate. But it will be better now.

Yosl led Dovid to his house, which was not far from the synagogue. Yosl instructed his maid to take Dovid's belongings and make up his room. Then Yosl led Dovid down a sloping hill outside of the town's limits. The pair walked for half an hour until they came to a large, bustling grain warehouse. The two men walked to Yosl's desk in the back of the warehouse where Yosl spent the afternoon explaining his current accounts and buy/sell agreements to Dovid.

In the beginning it was a mad, confusing blur to Dovid. He had difficulty following who was buying from whom, who was selling to whom, and who paid what to whom when, especially when there were all sorts of creditors tossing loans and promissory notes about in the middle. To his surprise, however, within a couple of days, Dovid found himself understanding the transactions much better. After a few weeks, he was developing bargaining strategies for Yosl to use with the Polish lords in whose grain he traded. After a few months it was Dovid who was negotiating with the Polish lords (although Yosl had to hire a tutor in Polish for him—Dovid's only language growing up had been Yiddish).

Yosl was delighted. Having watched his various sons move away to their fathers-in-law's houses and enter different businesses, he saw Dovid as the adopted son of his old age, who would protect and nurture Yosl's grain trading enterprise. Each day Yosl woke up with excitement to see what new insights Dovid had into the business. Yosl's profits soared.

While both men gloried in business, each was adrift when there was no business to do. During the week this was not a problem: They woke, plotted over breakfast, rushed through their morning prayers, and got to work. They went home together for dinner, and at the dinner table they debated business strategy some more. Yosl's daughter, Rachel, could often be seen sighing loudly, crossing her arms, and tapping her feet as the two men spoke of nothing but whether now was the time to lock His Excellency Count Such and Such into a price for his wheat, or instead to wait for the market to soften a bit and for the nobleman to panic as his gambling debts mounted. The two men paid no mind to Rachel.

But neither Yosl nor Dovid could bear the holy *Shabbat*. From Friday night to Saturday night they were prohibited from transacting business. Instead of feeling freed from worldly bonds to ascend to a special realm of holiness, the two men brooded. Their *Shabbat* table was lavish but deadly silent as neither man could think of anything to say. They shifted in their seats or asked how the dishes were prepared, although they did not really care.

Rachel did her best to expand her menfolk's horizons. She tried gossip: who was marrying whom, who was in a quarrel with whom, and so forth. Neither Dovid nor Yosl cared. They watched her lips moving, but her words soon became an indistinct hum of gurgling sounds. They would nod absently.

So Rachel tried a different tack. As a good Jewish household they had an obligation to invite poorer Jews to their *Shabbat* table, and so Rachel invited beggars and poor travelers to dine with them. The beggars, however, were intimidated by their rich hosts and ate silently, eyes facing down. Rachel thus found herself surrounded by more uncomfortably silent men. Moreover, one Saturday night, the maid discovered one of the beggars had made off with some silver utensils. Yosl promptly declared an end to inviting over the beggars. Rachel could make all the donations she liked to the community's charitable funds to feed and house these people, he said, but they were not entering his house again.

Thus Rachel tried something else: She invited over students from the nearby *yeshiva*. She let it be known that Yosl's home was open to all students of the Talmud who needed a meal on the *Shabbat*. The hungry students, who had trouble finding sponsors in town for all of their meals, eagerly jumped at the opportunity to eat at the table of the wealthy Yosl, and his home was soon swarming with budding scholars. For many of them, these *Shabbat* meals were the only meat they ate all week.

Words of Torah and debates about the thorniest Talmudic difficulties filled the air of Yosl's home as quotes from the *Mishnah* clashed with quotes from learned commentaries. Sometimes even mystical texts and esoteric doctrines were discussed. Rachel did not follow much of this discussion (as a girl, she was not permitted to learn the holy texts the way that boys did), but she felt the young scholars' words of Torah lifted her soul to an exalted state.

Yosl and Dovid, on the other hand, loathed the band of *yeshiva* students. For the life of him, Yosl could not imagine why they cared how animals were sacrificed in a temple in Jerusalem that had been reduced to rubble many centuries ago. Nor did he care about their abstruse debates regarding how the world began, how it would end, and how to reach the mystical godhead in its perfection and purity. As far as Yosl was concerned, the world had already begun long ago, without caring what these preening fools thought about it, and the world was not ending soon. So why all this racket? Since we are stuck where we are in this time and place, Yosl thought, we may as well try to get the best spread between the fixed acquisition price for a local lord's excess harvest and the fluctuating markets back west in Krakow or Frankfurt. When the Messiah finally does get around to redeeming the Jewish people, then there will be ample time to ponder the mysteries of creation. But until then …

Dovid, too, loathed the *yeshiva* students, but for a different reason. When their debates became particularly heated, one *yeshiva* student would accuse his opponent of being a secret adherent of the doctrines of the false Messiah, Sabbatai Zevi. This charge was always vehemently denied, and strained explanations would be offered as to why such and such a position could not, under any circumstances, be equated with Sabbatean doctrines. Then the *yeshiva* students would launch into their version of gossip—swapping rumors about which rabbis or wealthy merchants were reputed to be secret followers of Sabbatai Zevi, or what new excesses and sins had been committed by Sabbatai's followers in the lands of the Sultan of Turkey.

These discussions made Dovid squirm inside and bite his lip. He worked hard to appear bored when Sabbatean heresies were discussed, ostentatiously sighing or slouching in his seat and staring blankly at his fingernails. But the ruse was not always easy. In those fingernails an image would start to form, cloudy and formless at first, but soon the shapes of two sad, old Jews were visible. These souls, whom Dovid remained convinced were his true parents, would look upon him again with pleading eyes. They wanted to be raised from the dead. Sabbatai Zevi still lived, albeit as a Muslim under the Sultan's protection. These ghosts were sure he was still working on his messianic mission, in some secret way, and that soon, very soon, he would redeem the Jews, and raise them from the dead to be reunited with their Dovid. How could their Dovid listen to these sneering unbelievers deny the Messiah? If it were up to these arrogant know-it-alls, Dovid's parents would rot in their graves for who knows how many centuries.

Dovid, in his mind, told his parents to hush. He could not speak up for them now; it would do no good. They must stop making these demands. His parents' dear departed souls became quiet, and meekly looked down. They obeyed their son, who was now a budding merchant. They respected his worldly shrewdness. Nevertheless, Dovid could see their heartache, and he burned with hatred for the *yeshiva* students who hurt his pious, humble parents.

In fact, it was their inability to stand the clamoring *yeshiva* students that finally drove Yosl and Dovid into outright sin. The two men would excuse themselves from the table and retire to Yosl's study. They would open a page of the Talmud and place it between them as if they were studying it, but in reality they discussed nothing but business in passionate whispers. Thus the two men willfully desecrated the holiness of *Shabbat* by secretly engaging in business. So great was their wickedness that they soon looked forward to *Shabbat* as the time when they could formulate business strategies without having to worry about being interrupted.

Yosl loved Dovid as if Dovid were his own son. Yosl's actual sons had found their father's business to be quite dull, and instead, had immersed themselves in Talmudic studies funded by their father's profits. Yosl himself, like Dovid, was not learned, but had built his business during the chaos of the Chmielnicki rebellion against the Polish crown, when the Polish nobles had needed a clever man who could store, hide, and transport their grain through enemy lines, and who could move money between themselves and the rest of Europe. Yosl had only been a lowly clerk in a grain-trading firm when Chmielnicki's men had swooped into town and murdered his employer and his employer's family. Yosl had survived because Chmielnicki's Cossacks had found him passed out drunk in the grain silo, and they thought the sight of a drunken Jew moaning beneath dried tracks of his own splattered orange vomit so funny that they could not bring themselves to harm him.

Once Yosl had become a wealthy man, he was matched to the daughter of a now-impoverished, but long distinguished family of rabbis. While initially proud to have such a grand wife and awed by her learning (which easily exceeded his own), Yosl grew to regret this match. His wife treated him with contempt and did not consult him before making household decisions. If he tried to object, or even to question her decrees, she would first ignore him and then tell him brusquely to be quiet—in front of the children and the servants.

At his wife's direction, Yosl's sons were educated, and not cheaply, in all the intricacies of the Talmud and its commentaries. For malicious fun, Yosl's wife enjoyed asking her husband a question of ritual observance, which he would not know, and she and his sons would snicker together and exchange laughing glances as Yosl fumbled around the point and tried to maintain his dignity. Needless to say, Yosl's sons had no interest in their father's business affairs or the remarkable cunning that it had taken to buy and sell grain in a Poland filled with rebel Cossacks and invading armies from Russia and Sweden.

Yosl retreated into his work. He savored the company of gentiles, both noble and common, and unlearned Jews who managed or leased farmland and lived apart from the Jewish towns in isolated country villages. While Yosl initially took joy in entering the synagogue with his learned boys, he soon came to dread sitting with them, as they repeatedly corrected his poor Hebrew. Truth be told, Yosl shed few tears when he packed them off to their in-laws' houses after his wife had made fine matches for them with distinguished Jewish families.

Rachel came as a surprise child of his old age, and then Yosl's wife had died three years after Rachel was born, carried away by a violent fever. Offers to marry poured into the wealthy widower, backed by the general consensus that a young girl needed a mother to raise her properly. But Yosl had suffered enough with one wife, and swore he would not bring such a plague down upon his head again.

So instead of marrying, Yosl brought an elderly aunt to live with him. She helped with Rachel and was kind and deferential; the aunt was from Yosl's poor family and in awe of his wealth. Buoyed by this newfound respect at home, Yosl even attended synagogue more often, praying at the eastern wall with the other town notables.

The greatest joy of these years was little Rachel. Her face always lit up when she saw her papa. She had loathed her mother's constant reproofs for being messy and ill-mannered. Papa, however, was kind and sweet, and brought her little candies each day. He sat her on his lap and she would tell him all about the dogs, goats, and birds she had seen that day. Sometimes she fell asleep cataloguing the neighborhood animals, and her head drooped on Yosl's shoulder. He would stroke her hair and kiss the top of her head, mumbling a Ukrainian lullaby he had heard as a little boy.

As she grew older, Rachel would ask her father about his past and business. Yosl gladly told her of the times he had been cornered by Cossacks or Russian troops and had to talk his way out of prison (or worse), or of how the Polish lords managed their vast estates. Still, as she was a girl, there was a limit to how far Yosl was comfortable involving Rachel in his business.

Yosl yearned for a son with whom he could share his business. His own sons lived far away, and rarely wrote to him. Every so often he and Rachel would visit them, for a Passover *Seder* or the birth of a new child. These meetings were awkward. Yosl's sons and daughters-in-law would greet him respectfully, ask perfunctory questions about the health of a couple of notables in Yosl's town, sit Yosl in a corner with a full glass of brandy, and then ignore him.

Yosl would sit and drink and watch his grown sons as if he were looking through a brightly lit window into a stranger's house.

Yosl thus thought the Holy One, Blessed be He, had answered his prayers when Moshe persuaded him to take Dovid in, and Dovid had turned out to have such a fine mind for business. Yosl thought living with Dovid and Rachel together was the height of happiness. Yosl, however, worried about the future. How long would Dovid stay as an apprentice in his business? Would Dovid not want to run his own firm? At some point Dovid would want to get married and join his father-in-law's business. What would Yosl do then?

Yosl could not bear the thought of losing his Dovid. So, as Rachel was of marriageable age, Yosl suggested to Dovid that he marry Rachel. Dovid agreed at once. The two men told Rachel and her aunt, who were overjoyed that the happy little household could continue without losing either Dovid or Rachel to outside suitors.

The wedding was a simple affair. While Yosl paid for ample food for the entire town, including all of the poor, he did not hire a large wedding band or a famous wedding jester. He brought instead a few Ukrainian peasants in the area with fine singing voices who entertained the guests with sentimental songs about lost loves.

Yosl's sons were outraged at this match and boycotted the wedding. Who was this Dovid, they demanded to know in their letters? Who was his family? What kind of learning did he have? Was their senile father taken in by some greedy adventurer? Yosl replied calmly that Dovid was a fine young man and his right hand in business, the son he had always wished for. This unsubtle rebuke set off a new storm of angry letters from Yosl's sons about how this match to a nobody was a stain on the family, which could only hurt their children's—that is, Yosl's grandchildren's—chances of making appropriate matches.

Yosl laughed at the thought of his finely mannered sons and daughters-in-law agonizing over the shame brought upon their heads through association with Dovid by marriage. He soon looked forward to the new letters from his sons, increasingly hysterical as the wedding date neared. They painted pictures of sad, shaking matchmaker heads at the suggestion of marrying Yosl's grandchildren to this or that illustrious family. The letters finally petered out. But none of Yosl's sons attended the wedding.

Roughly a year after the wedding Nachman was born. When he turned three, little Nachman entered the elementary school, the *cheder*, like the other boys in the town. He was an indifferent student, however, more interested in mischief with his friends (they liked to put little stones in the shoes of the teacher's wife and watch her yell in pain when she tried to walk).

When Nachman was five years old, Moshe came to visit. Dovid only vaguely recollected him from years before. Moshe stepped into the house with a broad smile, although he had to bend down to make it through the doorway. Rachel handed Moshe a glass of freshly brewed tea. Yosl and Dovid gossiped a bit with Moshe about recent fluctuations in grain prices and rumors of oversupply from the German lands depressing the market.

When the conversation reached a natural pause, Moshe suddenly asked to see Nachman. Dovid walked with Moshe to the *cheder* and asked the teacher to bring Nachman outside for a minute. Nachman trotted outside the building with a guilty smirk on his face, as he had just fed ink to a mouse, which he and his friends had trapped in a corner. Moshe dropped down to his knees, so that he was close to eye level with Nachman, and quizzed Nachman on what he was studying. Nachman's answers were evasive and confused, mixing up certain of his Hebrew letters and mangling his quotes from the Bible. As the examination proceeded

Moshe's visage darkened and his tone became sharper. Nachman stared at his feet and kicked the dirt.

Moshe stood up and said he was finished. Dovid told Nachman to go back into the *cheder*. Moshe waited until Nachman had disappeared indoors again before he turned to Dovid and spoke:

You have betrayed me and broken your promise. I delivered everything I promised you—a job with Yosl, the hand of Yosl's daughter in marriage. All I asked in return was that you raise your first born son to be a scholar whom I could proudly marry to my daughter someday. But your son is a lout! He is an embarrassment. He cannot even keep his letters straight.

If you want to keep your wife and your business, you will live up to your end of our agreement. You will remove the boy from this *cheder*, and he will study with a private tutor I will send to you. In six months' time I will test the boy again, and I will expect improvement. Fail to keep your word again and you will lose what I have so generously given you.

Dovid listened to this tirade without moving a muscle; he was alternately frightened and confused. He looked into Moshe's hot, blazing eyes and was not sure what to say. He started a sentence, then stopped, paused, and started again, before faltering once more. Finally, he spoke, catching his choked breaths here and there:

Moshe, what are you saying? All those years ago, I hardly remember, that was all a joke, right? You had drunk too much. I am sure your daughter will grow up to be beautiful and pious and have many suitors. We have no reason to quarrel.

Moshe replied, calmly and slowly:

That was no joke. You and I made a pact. I have honored it. You have not. I leave today. In three days' time, I will send the tutor. I will return myself in six months. Then I will judge whether you have lived up to our bargain.

Moshe went away. Three days later a young man, tall, lean, and painfully well-mannered, presented himself at Dovid's house. The young man handed a letter to Dovid. It read:

To my fine and true friend Dovid,
The bearer of this letter is the tutor for your son. Remember your promise.
With warmest affection,
Moshe

Dovid sat down uneasily on a large, soft chair. The young man stood politely and silently, with his arms folded behind his back and his eyes fixed on some distant point. The two men were alone.

Dovid considered the letter. All this talk of a pact is absurd, he told himself. Moshe had been a rambling drunkard that night. Dovid even had trouble recalling what was said, as everything was so long ago. And what could Moshe do to him?

Still, one never knew. Perhaps, Dovid pondered, Moshe would speak ill of him. As Dovid was emerging from behind Yosl to establish himself as a merchant in his own right, it would not be good to have an enemy spreading slander.

And perhaps Moshe was right? Nachman did not seem to be learning much in the *cheder* and was hardly a boy that a father could take much pride in. Maybe Moshe was helping Dovid again? Moshe had convinced Yosl to hire Dovid. Perhaps this was another good turn by Moshe? Regardless, how much less could Nachman learn anyway? Why not try the tutor for a while? The *cheder* was not going anywhere and would always take back a pupil whose father paid the full tuition and paid it promptly. The young man is here, Dovid concluded, let's try him out.

So Dovid hired the young man and pulled Nachman out of the *cheder*. His wife and father-in-law protested at first—who was this tutor? What was so wrong with the *cheder*? Wouldn't Nachman miss his friends?

After a week, all doubts were dispelled. Nachman wanted nothing more than to study day and night with his tutor. He learned rapidly and soon more than caught up to where he should have been. He stopped asking for his friends and ignored them when they came around on *Shabbat*.

When Moshe returned for another visit six months later, he was delighted at Nachman's progress. He quizzed the boy again, but this time with a smile and gentle, encouraging words. After Nachman passed the impromptu examination with perfect marks, Moshe gave the boy a handful of sweets.

Moshe pulled Dovid aside:

You have kept your promise. I will check back every few months. Each time I come and see that you are keeping your word, I will give you a gift. Now I give you a daughter, in your Rachel's womb, and a business opportunity.

And so it came to pass: Six weeks later Rachel told Dovid she was pregnant, and seven months later she gave birth to Hannah. At about the same time he learned of Rachel's pregnancy, Dovid was summoned to the manor of the wealthiest landowner in the area with whom he did a small amount of business here and there. The magnate announced to Dovid, quite out of the blue, that he had decided from then on to do business with only one grain merchant and that would be Dovid. The profits from this contract more than doubled the size of Yosl's business.

The pattern was soon established: Every few months Moshe would visit Dovid, assess Nachman's scholarly progress, and promise a gift—a promise always followed by a new child or a new business success.

Yosl eventually passed away from this world. Moshe attended the funeral and promised afterwards that Dovid's inheritance would be protected. Dovid was not so sanguine: With Dovid's skill and Moshe's strange blessings, Yosl's grain trading firm had swollen in size and profitability, and Rachel's brothers lodged lawsuits contesting Yosl's will to get their hands on it. However, as Moshe promised, these suits failed; and in one instance the litigious brother was even forced to pay damages back to Dovid.

Dovid grew convinced Moshe was no ordinary man, but possessed magical powers. At first, Dovid thought Moshe was a *lamed-vovnik*, a hidden saint, but then he recalled that the thirty-six hidden saints lived in humble poverty, whereas Moshe was a wealthy merchant who wore fine clothes and indulged in expensive wines.

So Dovid decided Moshe must be an angel sent from Paradise to guide him and Nachman towards some special destiny. Maybe, Dovid thought, his righteous, natural parents, whose ghosts once haunted him, had beseeched the Throne of Glory for a benevolent decree for their poor orphan. The Heavenly Tribunal must have granted their wish and sent Moshe to Earth as the angel to carry out the divine decree.

V. The Temptation of Dovid

AS TIME PASSED, Dovid no longer needed more money, nor could he wish for more children. And such wonderful children: Nachman grew each day into a greater scholar. While Dovid could not follow his son's abstruse discourse, he liked to listen in on Nachman's chanting of the Talmud or his debates with his tutors; Dovid felt a rush of warmth each time Nachman made a point with confidence. Dovid was forever embarrassing Nachman in front of strangers with extravagant praise for the boy's genius, and he loved to grab Nachman from behind at the kitchen table and kiss his cheek.

But Nachman the scholar was impatient with these earthly affections, and would brush off his father's expressions of love. Dovid's eldest daughter Hannah, on the other hand, reveled in her father's attention. Dovid enjoyed sitting with her on long, lazy *Shabbat* afternoons or in the hour before dinner each night, when he would regale her with his business adventures. Hannah would smile and prod her father for more. Sometimes she would surprise him with little gifts she made herself—a handkerchief she sewed, or an old *yarmulke* she mended and redecorated to her taste. Dovid would proudly display these items as he walked through the town and rained fury upon any onlooker who dared snicker at Hannah's craftsmanship.

The one sore point in Dovid's life was that Rachel had grown distant. When they were first married she embraced him often and would impatiently count the days when her monthly impurity would end so she could rush to the *mikveh* (ritual bath) to cleanse herself and lay with her Dovid again.

But Rachel's passion cooled with each year and each new child. Running the household, with its children and servants, became an ever heavier burden and sapped her energy. Rachel still loved her Dovid and wanted to satisfy him, but there was only so much she could do. Embracing her husband went from passion to chore, and then to a chore to be ducked and avoided. Rachel now tried to lengthen her period of impurity and delayed cleansing herself in the *mikveh*. She reveled in her newfound piety.

Rachel pushed her husband away. She pleaded with him that she was assailed by sufferings in many parts of her body—stomach cramps, headaches, arthritic hands, sore feet—and she needed to rest and get better—could he not wait just a while longer? Not tonight, but soon? The gaps between one soon and the next lengthened over time.

And when her father Yosl died, Rachel lost all joy in life. During the prescribed seven days of mourning she would not leave her bed and she barely ate. In the weeks that followed Rachel sleepwalked through the day with puffy, distant eyes. Her dresses now resembled wrinkled tents on her withering pole of a body. Rachel even ignored her children and gave them free rein to eat sweets and to neglect their chores. While the children (save Nachman, who spent his days squirreled away with his tutors and Talmud tractates) were thrilled with their newfound freedom, their mother's indifference eventually lent a heavy air of sadness and quiet worry to their games.

Dovid tried to comfort Rachel. He added an extra servant to lighten her burdens. He thought it must be terrible to have known and loved a parent that long, and then to lose him; as an orphan, Dovid was painfully aware of his inability to understand her suffering. Dovid himself was reeling from Yosl's death; Yosl had been a surrogate father for him. But he knew it was different for Rachel, and moreover, he had the business to manage, which forced his mind to focus on other matters.

Dovid sat down next to her on the sofa in the parlor one warm, sun-drenched *Shabbat* afternoon when the house was empty except for the two of them. He grabbed her hand and whispered she was a wonderful woman, a good wife and daughter and mother, but this sadness could not last forever. She had children to raise, and a household to run. Her father, Yosl, may his memory be a blessing, was no doubt in Paradise in the World to Come, negotiating with the holy sages how he would supply grain to the cities of the Holy Land when the Messiah should come. Who knows, Dovid continued, perhaps he has even met my parents and put in a good word for me, too …

Rachel had not looked at Dovid as he spoke, but stared blankly towards a thick, creamy white curtain, which dulled the dazzling sunlight outside. She now turned her head to Dovid and looked at him for a long time with a puzzled expression. She appeared to Dovid to be trying to figure out who he was and what he was doing next to her on the sofa.

Suddenly, Rachel pulled her hand away. She arched her back like a vicious cat and twisted her body away from her husband. She snapped at him: Stop it, go away. Don't touch me.

Dovid sat dumbstruck and did not know what to do. He groped for a word, but before he could find one, a sharp, shrill *get out* knocked him over and he stumbled out the door.

Worse troubles were to come. Rachel realized soon after this fight with her husband that she was pregnant again. She wanted nothing to do with any life at this point, much less a new life, and tried to hide the pregnancy. However, as with each pregnancy, Rachel suffered from terrible nausea each morning, and Dovid soon realized he had another child on the way. He beamed; he was sure a new baby, with its soft skin and little feet, would bring Rachel back into the sunlight. Dovid thought Rachel must realize, sooner or later, that, until the Messiah comes to redeem Israel and to raise the dead, it is to be expected that some die and then others are born.

One late afternoon Dovid came home to a gruesome sight. Dovid saw Rachel stretched out on the sofa, looking more dead than alive; her body was covered in sweat and her crumpled, damp dress stuck tightly to her thin, wasting frame. Her eyes were wide open but had no expression and seemed to Dovid to be staring down the shaft of an invisible well.

The servants were scrubbing the floors—there was blood everywhere. A group of clucking women, small, bent, and with ill-fitting greasy wigs, hovered about. One of them noticed Dovid and motioned him aside. She whispered:

Poor girl, she lost the baby. This is no place for a husband now. We will take care of her. Come back later.

Dovid nodded and silently left. He spent the rest of the day inspecting and organizing shipments of newly harvested grain. He worked hard not to think about his dead child.

Later that night, after the children had been put to bed, Dovid approached Rachel. He told himself he should try to comfort her. A little tenderness, he thought, and she would snap out of this; she would realize life is about the living, not the dead. So he sat next to her on her bed, picked up her hand, and lightly stroked it.

Rachel pulled her hand away. Don't touch me, she hissed.

Dovid stood up and backed away. He thought, what more can I do? I have tried to be a good husband, but there is no pleasing Rachel anymore. I am hateful in her eyes; my touch is like acid on her skin—but why? What have I done to deserve this?

Dovid's rage began to well up. She was supposed to be his support, his helpmeet, and here he was begging for a small stale crust of her affection—and she denied him even that? Did she not owe him obligations of love and support in the marriage contract, the *ketubah*, she had signed? She had broken her oath and sinned. Now the words flowed out of Dovid's mouth without him realizing it:

How dare you? You signed our *ketubah* promising to be a true wife to me, and now you scorn me like a slab of maggot-infested *treyf* meat. You have a duty to me, and to your children. Your father, may he rest in peace, has left this world for the world to come. Just like everyone must. You had many good years with him, for which you should thank the Holy One, Blessed be He, for His kindness. My parents fell at the hands of Chmielnicki's murderers before I could know them. Yet I have managed to put one foot in front of the other.

But you, you have moped and moaned and neglected your health and well-being. And you can see the result—you killed the baby inside you. You have never lost a child before, but this time you neglected to eat and take care of yourself, and you killed our child. I am sure that little soul is now weeping with your father in the world to come, and your father is cursing you to the saints and sages as a murderer. I am finished pretending you are a decent wife and mother, you are a disgusting, wretched sinner, a murderer, and you need to beg my forgiveness.

Dovid stormed out of the house and slept in his grain silo. He did not speak to his wife until two days later, when he abruptly informed her he needed to travel on business over the next few weeks. He would, unfortunately, be away on the *Sukkoth* holiday, but business is business. He would write to her when he had a chance.

Rachel said nothing. She looked down, appearing to Dovid as if she felt ashamed of something. By the time she had raised her head again Dovid was gone.

Dovid traveled several towns over, to pay a visit to a Polish lord whose grain he had contracted to purchase at the beginning of the summer. As the harvest had come in, Dovid went to settle accounts. Dovid enjoyed the carriage ride through the countryside. The weather had yet to turn cold, and the sun spread lovingly over the grain fields and the birch trees. Dovid recognized many of the peasants and small landowners with whom he did business. He was comfortable with them; he knew they looked at him as a dirty Christ-killing Yid, but as dirty Christ-killing Yids went they found him alright. He was honest, put on no airs, and always carried a small bottle of vodka to share. Dovid waved to these friends; they waved back. He emptied himself of all thought and concentrated on the sun and trees and fields.

It was late at night when Dovid reached his destination, where he took a room at the local inn. Dovid sat down at a wobbly wooden table in the inn's front area and ordered some borscht for dinner. A large man approached him from behind. Dovid swiveled around and saw, much to his surprise, his old friend Moshe.

May I join you? I am also passing through on business.

Dovid motioned for him to sit down. Moshe called over the waitress and ordered vodka, but no food. The two men spoke and drank. In the beginning, the talk was the normal talk of merchants on the road: the weather, the inn, recent business deals, grain prices, gossip about competitors.

As they drank more, Moshe grew bolder. You seem troubled somehow, he said, unburden yourself. Maybe I can offer some advice.

Dovid first denied there was anything wrong, but as the night wore on and the vodka flowed freely in his veins he found himself relating his domestic troubles—Rachel's refusal to be a wife to him, her unending despair at Yosl's death, the miscarriage and Dovid's harsh words.

Moshe looked kindly at Dovid in the dim candlelight and offered his counsel:

Dovid, do not be so harsh with Rachel. It is hard to be a wife and mother. She has many burdens—children, household chores, the judgmental nattering of the other women in town, and then on top of all that to lose a father and a child, no wonder she despairs. And you dared to attack her character? It is you who should beg her forgiveness.

Here is what you should do: Go home. You know this trip is just an excuse to avoid her. Apologize and beg her forgiveness for your cruel words. But you must also commit to stop being a burden to her. You must lighten her load, too. You are a man, I am a man, and we both know men need what we need. If you insist on taking that from Rachel, this fighting will never end—she will deny you, and your blood will boil with frustration and hate. Your *shalom bayit*, your domestic peace, will shatter. You know the importance our holy sages have placed on *shalom bayit* and maintaining the harmony between a husband and a wife.

So stop demanding of Rachel what she can no longer give you. You have a pretty, young Ukrainian maid, Maryska. I know her family; their village is not far from a lord with whom I do business sometimes. That family is always in trouble. The father drinks away every coin, and Maryska's mother must scramble to keep her children fed and her hut warm. See, you have needs Maryska can help with, and she has needs where you can help. Strike the right bargain and everyone is happy—your *shalom bayit* is preserved, and Maryska's family will have food and firewood for the hard winter.

Dovid was, by this time, quite drunk. Moshe's words echoed and bounced around his head slowly and loudly. He thought for a few moments and then slurred:

But isn't this forbidden? Are you suggesting I sin?

Moshe smiled:

You are no scholar. You are unlearned, so naturally you think in such simple terms. There will be sin here no matter what. You and Rachel can mistreat each other, and you will each sin. That is the road you have been hopping along for some time. Or you can save Rachel from sin, and yourself from a greater sin, by doing a little sin, and a little sin that will also help feed a family. So a sin mixed with a *mitzvah*, a good deed. Speaking of what is permitted and what is forbidden is fine for most situations, but sometimes you must choose the lesser sin. Have I ever steered you wrong? Listen to me again now. Avoid the greater sin of destroying a good Jewish home.

Dovid would never remember how or when he fell asleep that night. The next day he dutifully kept his appointment with the Polish lord and conducted his business. His mind, however, kept wandering to Maryska. She was young, with flat, dry, long blonde hair. Living in Dovid's house she had grown slightly plump. Dovid thought restlessly of her wide hips and her breasts struggling against her flimsy, grease-stained blouses. Her movements were harsh and clumsy, he reflected, but he suddenly found himself unable to stop thinking about her.

These thoughts kindled guilt and shame. Dovid reflected, however, that if Rachel had only done her duty as his wife, his fevered brain would not be drawn to such filth. These sinful thoughts were not really his fault but hers—what else could she expect a scorned husband, still in his prime, to think about?

By the time his business was concluded Dovid had decided to follow Moshe's advice. Moshe himself was nowhere to be seen;

Dovid learned from the innkeeper that Moshe had continued on his way the morning after their talk. No matter, Dovid thought, I shall thank him at a later time. It is good to have such a learned and kind friend.

Dovid returned home much earlier than expected, arriving just past dinner time. Rachel was rustling the children into bed and Maryska was cleaning off the table. The children were excited to see their father home, especially Hannah, who ran over and kissed her papa on the cheek and showed him some of his socks she had mended. Dovid hugged her tightly, and he was surprised to feel tears falling upon his cheek. He had missed his Hannah.

Rachel said nothing and looked away. Dovid did not approach her yet, but instead urged the children to go with their mother for their bedtime routine. Dovid watched them walk away, a group of obedient little ducklings led by their mother.

After they left he stood in the dining room alone with Maryska. Dovid removed his coat, and placed it on a nearby chair, without looking too closely at what he was doing. He watched Maryska gather up the plates into one big pile in the corner of the table. She muttered something in Ukrainian but Dovid did not understand her. She yawned, rubbed her eyes, and then organized the glasses into a separate pile. She stood back and stared at her handiwork and then yawned again. Maryska turned to grab hold of the plate pile when she finally noticed Dovid staring at her.

I am so sorry sir, she said, can I get you some tea? Tea is good on a cold night after a journey. Maryska forced a slight smile.

Dovid felt his body begin to sweat. His throat choked up, and his mind turned into a blur—suddenly, he could not find the strength to answer whether he wanted a cup of tea. He finally squeezed out a barely audible yes, thank you, please, very much.

Relieved there was no further question to answer, Dovid sat down on a chair by the table and steadied himself. Maryska nodded, grabbed the plates, and went off to the kitchen. She mumbled some more in Ukrainian. Dovid watched her walk away. Her steps are clumsy, he thought, and her gait is heavy, like an old, fat horse stuck again to the same beat-up wagon. She has none of Rachel's easy, light grace.

Still, Dovid could not stop looking at her hair. Rachel, like all good Jewish wives, hid her hair—under wigs, under kerchiefs tied in knots under her chin. Dovid always loved women's hair, and when Yosl first betrothed him to Rachel he would stare longingly at her long, curly brown hair. In the early years of their marriage, Dovid grew excited when he was finally alone with his Rachel, and she would slowly remove her wig, and he could see her gorgeous hair. But, Dovid sighed, it had been many months since he had seen Rachel's hair. Maryska's hair was not as wondrous as Rachel's hair—while long, it was flat and fell on her back in straight, damp clumps. Yet Dovid could not stop looking at it.

Maryska returned with his tea, placing the glass and the bowl of sugar cubes gently down in front of him. Dovid felt his temples throb and his throat tighten again. He smiled uncomfortably. He picked up a sugar cube, but dropped it on the table by accident. Maryska picked up the sugar cube and put it back in his hand. She let her fingers linger on his hand, and she looked hard at him with a wrinkled brow and alert eyes. Dovid felt guilty about having physical contact with a woman who was not his wife. He felt he had committed a terrible sin, and he snatched his hand away. Maryska laughed, mumbled again in Ukrainian, and returned to the kitchen. Dovid drank a couple of quick sips of tea, although he forgot to put the sugar in the glass. He walked up the stairs still carrying the sugar cube in his hand.

Once upstairs, Dovid found Rachel lying in her bed, although she was wide awake. The sight of her filled him with shame. Dovid felt at that moment Rachel was the finest, the most goodly, Jewish wife in the world—she was a saint, an angel, and he was a wretched, disgusting lecher.

Dovid fell down next to her bedside and cried. Rachel sat up, startled, and looked at him. Once he pulled himself together, Dovid told Rachel he had sinned against her and begged her forgiveness. He told her he had met Moshe on his trip, and Moshe had opened his eyes to Dovid's failures to live up to his duty as a husband. He had come home early because he had to unburden himself and seek her forgiveness.

Rachel put her arms around her Dovid's head. She kissed the top of his head, and in a calm voice, told him not to worry, things would be better. She gently urged him to go to sleep; after all, he must be tired from his travels.

Dovid went to his bed, feeling light and happy. He swore to himself he would be a good husband, and would pay no more attention to Maryska or Moshe's silly drunken theories of greater sins and lesser sins. Satisfied with himself, Dovid closed his eyes and welcomed the sweet blackness of sleep.

Over the next few weeks Rachel and Dovid reached an equilibrium. They were polite to each other, even friendly. Dovid would greet her in the morning, and they would each discuss their plans for the day. At night, over dinner, Dovid would dryly recite the facts of his day—people and lands visited, bushels bought, sold, and hedged, bookkeeping entries reconciled—in a steady monotone. Rachel smiled and listened, and then commented upon some domestic matter—either the good or the bad behavior of a child, say, or how she realized they needed to polish their candlesticks soon, before *Shabbat*. Dovid would nod in turn and praise his wife's fine judgment.

Maryska, meanwhile, was busy moving plates, glasses, and food in and out of the kitchen. She did not speak, but every so often glared at Dovid out of the corner of her eye. Dovid hated those looks. He would invariably stumble on his words when Maryska's eyes landed on him. Dovid knew Maryska was taunting him, but he was terrified of her at the same time.

Dovid was haunted by Maryska. He would remember Moshe's advice, crazy, sinful advice, and find himself staring at her. Maryska would notice Dovid's stare and ask if he needed anything. He would usually ask for tea and then forget to drink it.

Dovid felt Maryska flaunted her newfound power over him. She would approach him with slow, confident steps, lean her body close to his, and let her hair fall on him, as if by accident. Or she would let the hem of her dress brush up against him. Dovid reacted by staring down at the floor, focusing on a spot where he could not see her. Still, he felt her breath on the back of his neck and smelled the garlic stench she carried from the kitchen. Dovid felt relieved at the end of each day when nothing had happened with Maryska. Each night, he swore to himself as he went to bed that he would let Maryska go the next morning. Yet somehow he could not bring himself to throw her out of his house.

One evening Dovid worked late in his grain silo. A Polish lord had complained of being shortchanged on the sale of His Excellency's grain to the markets in the West, so Dovid knew a thorough accounting would be demanded. With a sigh and several good candles, he sat down to work with his receipts and ledgers, to make sure his records were in order. He expected a summons to the lord's manor house any day, and he needed to be ready. Alone at his desk in the cavernous, dusty building, Dovid toiled as the sun slowly faded outside, and the sky blurred from blue to red to black.

In the evening, Dovid heard the door creaking and then heavy plodding footsteps. He jumped up; he was scared this could be his summons to His Excellency and there were still certain accounting entries to reconcile. Dovid grabbed at his papers and tried to organize them, but found himself dropping one paper as he reached for another.

The heavy footsteps approached. Dovid did not look up, but dived to the ground to organize the scattered records. He was certain he had everything, but where was the record of the grain shipment last Wednesday—was it there?—no, over here—or there?

And then there was laughter. What stunned Dovid was not so much that he was being laughed at, but that the voice was feminine. His Excellency would not have sent a woman to fetch him. So Dovid looked up.

There was Maryska. She was carrying a package, which she placed on an empty corner of his desk. Dovid smelled herring and onions, no doubt with black bread: a package from Rachel to help him keep body and soul stitched together. Dovid did not move, but looked up at her in the half-light of the candles.

Maryska removed her kerchief and let her hair fall down. She walked slowly over to Dovid until she stood right over him. Then she bent down until her face hovered just above his, and she let her hair fall on his cheeks. Dovid neither moved nor spoke.

Poor sir, she said, you look so tired and sad. You work so hard, but nobody takes care of you.

Dovid remained silent, but his eyes were fixed upon Maryska's face.

I could help you, she continued. I could take care of you. The mistress does not take care of you the way a wife should.

Maryska reached out and took hold of Dovid's hands. She pulled him up and led him into a corner area of the silo, in between crates and sacks, where the candlelight did not reach. In the dark corner, amidst moldy rotted grain stalks that had not been worth selling, Dovid committed many sins.

Maryska left when they were done. She said nothing, but her steps were lighter and she hummed something to herself in

Ukrainian. Dovid returned to his desk. He decided not to think about what had just happened and devoted himself ever more energetically to his work. He did not touch the dinner Maryska had brought.

Dovid eventually fell asleep on his desk. His clerks woke him when they arrived the next morning, and Dovid pulled himself together again and started for home. On the way, he told himself he had not been in his right mind the previous night, and what happened with Maryska was not his fault—she had started it, and he did not even really enjoy the sin. He promised himself from now on he would be a good husband, a perfect husband to Rachel, and he would dismiss Maryska that morning.

When he reached his door, Dovid felt a terrible throbbing in his skull and a slight dizziness. He went inside and fell onto the sofa. Hannah brought him some water to drink. Dovid could not look her in the eye.

Rachel returned a few minutes later. She was alarmed at the sight of Dovid and hustled him off to bed. She scolded him playfully for working too hard. Dovid told her she was the finest, the most caring wife a man could wish for, he did not deserve her, and he was so sorry he had hurt her before. Hush, Rachel said, rest, and stop talking nonsense.

Dovid woke several hours later. The Polish lord had sent a messenger for him, but left upon hearing Dovid was ill in bed. Dovid sat up and rubbed his eyes. He felt calm; it was as if his sin had never happened. The previous night seemed unreal.

Maryska came in with a tray of tea and honey cake, which she placed it next to the bed. Once again, Maryska towered above the sitting Dovid. Her physical presence, those lazy wide hips and falling hair and breasts pressing against flimsy fabric, made Dovid tense and excited and angry and ashamed all at once.

Now, Dovid thought, cast her from your house. As Abraham cast out Hagar, so cast out this sinful maidservant who has come between you and your wife. She is not even pretty—she is a fat, clumsy cow. Why would you risk losing this world and the world to come over a fat clumsy cow?

But he could not bring himself to speak the words. He saw her hands and longed again to feel them grab him. No, he told himself, no more sinful thoughts. Cast her away to her village.

However, a new thought crossed his mind: Should he cast Maryska away, what would stop Maryska from telling everything to Rachel? Even accusing him of being the aggressor? He could not risk it. Dovid did not trust in his ability to lie about his sin if Rachel confronted him directly. So Maryska must stay.

Don't feel guilty, sir, Maryska said softly. A man needs things every so often.

Maryska left. Dovid washed, dressed, returned to the silo, gathered his papers, and instructed his coachman to take him to the lord's estate, to answer the summons. Dovid spent the evening at His Excellency's manor and was able to iron out his business difficulties. Dovid returned home relieved.

With each passing day, Dovid's sin with Maryska seemed less real, and he even doubted sometimes whether it had really happened. Maybe it was a dream? All those fevered ideas Moshe had planted had resulted in a mad, sinful dream, but it was only a dream. It must be a dream: How could Dovid have committed such a sin and the world continued on its merry way without noticing? Rachel was the same, the children were the same, business was the same. This sameness was conclusive proof to Dovid that nothing had actually happened.

Dovid found himself alone with Maryska one morning. He had slept late, and Rachel had sent Maryska to his room with tea and bread and plum preserves. Maryska leaned close to Dovid and stretched her chest and arms over his body as she slowly lay the tray down, but she did not touch him.

Dovid felt a surge of desire. He wanted to touch Maryska, his heart palpitated, and he felt lightheaded. Without thinking he reached up and grabbed Maryska's arm. She smiled and brushed off his weak grip.

Poor sir. Not here. Tonight, at your silo. Go there after dinner and wait. I will come to you.

Maryska walked away, whistling, with heavy, banging steps.

The day was torture for Dovid. He found himself asking his clerks to repeat what they said; everyone seemed to speak too quickly that day. Images of Maryska bubbled up in Dovid's mind without respite, although he willed himself to suppress them. He swore to himself he would not go to meet her that night. He would do the right thing and be a good husband.

Dovid barely kept his composure through dinner. Despite having no appetite he forced himself to eat. Dovid could not look at either Rachel or Maryska, and so focused his attention upon Nachman, asking his son to explain what he was studying, and to bless the gathering with words of Torah. Nachman obliged, and commenced a lengthy, monotone explanation of the passage he was studying, the views of different commentators, and Nachman's own thoughts on how to resolve the difficulties in the text. Dovid prodded Nachman to flesh out his explanations in ever more minute detail. While Dovid had almost no understanding of Nachman's abstruse discourse, he found the sound of his son's learned, chaste words to be soothing.

Before Dovid knew it, the dishes were being cleared. He stood up and told Rachel he had some business to attend to at the grain silo. Rachel nodded and teased him about working so hard. Dovid walked rapidly, almost ran, to the silo. As he went, Dovid thought, this is wrong, I should turn back, I can still turn back.

But he continued forward.

The silo was empty and still. Dovid walked to his desk and lit a small candle, which cast a weak, trembling orange light. Dovid told himself to leave but felt his body was frozen in place.

Dovid lost track of time. His mind whirled between images of Maryska and images of Rachel. To calm himself, he focused his mind on the faint sound of water dripping slowly.

Maryska came. She walked up to Dovid, gently held his hand, and led him back to a dark, moldy corner. Once again, Dovid sinned.

This time Maryska did not leave afterwards, but spoke to Dovid:

Sir, I have a favor to ask. My family, back in my village, needs help. My father drinks away all the money, and there is nothing left for food and boots. Can you give me some extra money? It can be our little secret. It would mean a lot to me, sir, and you would be helping good people.

Dovid hesitated. To sin was bad enough, but to pay the woman afterwards seemed somehow much worse. But maybe, he thought, she was telling the truth. Perhaps she did have a family that needed help.

Dovid looked at her. His eyes had become acclimated to the dark, and he believed he saw an expression of hope and longing. Dovid was suddenly scared of disappointing Maryska and felt a powerful desire to keep her happy, even though he told himself he should not care.

So Dovid went to the safe and gave her some money. Maryska thanked him and left.

Thus, a pattern emerged: Dovid would try to resist his desires, convince himself he had conquered his evil inclination, his *yetzer hara*, and devote himself ever more zealously to Rachel. He would surprise his wife with gifts of jewelry and shower her with compliments. Dovid told himself he and Rachel were closer than ever.

With his courage built up, Dovid would approach Rachel at night in her bed. But she always pushed him away. Sometimes she offered reasons—a headache, exhaustion from chasing the children, worry about something she had to do—but other times she just rolled over in her bed.

Dovid would sigh and walk back to his bed, feeling acutely the humiliation of his defeat. He would lie down, but be unable to sleep. Rachel snored, and each loud groan seemed to Dovid to be a laugh at his weakness.

Self-pity would turn to hate: He had, Dovid said to himself, been nothing but an excellent husband, so why was Rachel spurning him so cruelly? What had he done to merit such treatment at his wife's hands? Was she not breaking the terms of the marriage contract and thus sinning against him?

Yes, he told himself, she was sinning against him. Maryska was right—he was a man and he had needs, and Rachel was acting wrongfully.

The next morning Dovid would arrange another nocturnal meeting with Maryska, who never turned him down. The tryst was always followed by a new wave of remorse, and a new attempt by Dovid to win Rachel's favor. Maryska patiently snickered in the background as she watched Dovid try to prove to himself that he was, after all, a good husband.

Dovid's meetings with Maryska grew more frequent. Still, she never refused him. But Maryska's demands for money grew ever greater. She stopped justifying them with tales of her family's woes and simply told Dovid to fetch this or that sum. Maryska spoke now with the perfect confidence of someone who expects to be obeyed.

Terrified that she may refuse to see him again, Dovid gave Maryska everything she demanded. He worried that in the near future his expenditures on Maryska could begin to outstrip his earnings, ample though they were. Dovid cast about desperately for a means to raise more money.

He tried to squeeze his workers, stinting on their wages while demanding longer hours. This backfired: His best workers quit, and Dovid found himself making less money than ever. He was forced to beg his good workers to return, and he had to raise their wages higher than before—thus making his predicament even worse.

Dovid owned the land where his grain silos were located and took a mortgage out on the property to pay Maryska. Yet she demanded more. When Dovid balked, Maryska refused her favors and furiously swore she would not see Dovid again alone at night until he had met her demands.

Dovid told himself this was a blessing: Now that Maryska's demands had reached a point he could not satisfy, Dovid would be forced to stop sinning. Perhaps this was the way of the Holy One, Blessed be He, to lead wretched Dovid back to the right path?

For a few days Dovid felt relieved, even liberated. He was sure of himself and his return to virtue. He was kinder to his children and to his workers. He praised Rachel at every opportunity—everything she did was wondrous, from caring for the children to picking furniture to preparing honey cakes. Dovid hoped Maryska would quit and leave his house, as he still lacked the will to dismiss her.

But Maryska did not leave. To the contrary, she made a point of hovering close to Dovid, although she did not speak to him or touch him. The sight of her was constantly before his eyes, and soon his desires overpowered him once more. He had to be with her again. But how? Her price was so high.

One afternoon Dovid was pacing around his grain silo, alone, his mind bombarded by these terrible desires and frustrations. He sat down on a nearby stool feeling helpless and staring forward at the sacks of grain. He saw no way out of his misery.

And looking at the sacks of grain, he found his solution.

Dovid spent the rest of the day and the night emptying the top third of each grain sack and putting that grain into different sacks, which he would fill only two-thirds. Once he had a warehouse of two-thirds-full bags, Dovid put filler—weeds, chaff, grass—into the sacks and mixed them artfully with the real grains, such that each two-thirds-full bag appeared to be completely full of grain. Dovid sold the fraudulent bags as full bags of grain, and this deceit led to a boom in his profits—more than enough to pay off Maryska, who was now eager again to sin with him.

All Dovid could think about was how to keep Maryska happy. He brought his tricks to the purchase side of his business, rigging his weights to make it appear there was less grain in the sacks he bought than there really was. Dovid's profits swelled, and he poured these ill-gotten gains into Maryska's fat, sweaty fingers.

Dovid lost patience for everything but Maryska. The synagogue filled him with boredom and disgust. As a hypocrite himself who mouthed the prayers but longed for sin, he assumed those around him were equally focused upon sin, and he scorned them for their hypocrisy, and excused his own as no worse than anyone else's.

Dovid compared Rachel unfavorably to Maryska: Rachel was cold, fragile, and thin, more a wraith than a woman, whereas Maryska was hot-blooded and fleshy and curvy. He had no patience for Rachel anymore, and he was irritated when she tried to speak to him: Haven't I enough troubles in business without your nagging, he would snap at her. Don't bother me with your nonsense. I slave each day at my business, and all you do is take the wealth I make and act like it is all yours. And then you want to rob me of my few moments of rest with stupid questions.

Rachel stopped speaking much to her husband. She became scared of him for the first time and, also for the first time in their marriage, her Dovid did not even try to touch her in any way. He avoided her at night, and now every night he was going out to the grain silo after dinner.

But what prompted Rachel to act was his treatment of the children. He no longer heaped boundless praise upon Nachman, but berated him as a parasite who sucked Dovid's blood with his expensive private tutors. Dovid was even crueler to Hannah. Where before he had always had long talks with her and made a slight fool of himself strutting about town displaying Hannah's handcrafts proudly upon his person, now Dovid often refused to speak to Hannah, shouting at her to get out of his way and to leave him alone.

One night, as Dovid was about to leave for yet another visit after dinner to the grain silo, Hannah had remembered she had made an embroidered *tallit* bag that day as a surprise gift for her father. She ran up to Dovid and said, don't go papa—I have a special surprise for you, please stay tonight, your work can wait.

Dovid ignored her and continued to put his coat on.

Please papa, I made you something, please stay, please. Just tonight.

Dovid said nothing.

Hannah grabbed Dovid's leg. I am not letting go until you agree to stay home tonight.

Get off me. I have to go.

No, you are staying home tonight. That is final. No more work.

Dovid glared down. He was perfectly still for a moment. Hannah's face began to brighten. But then Dovid raised his foot, the one that Hannah had grabbed hold of, and kicked her across the room. He stormed out.

Hannah ran to her bed and sobbed. She grabbed the *tallit* bag and tore it up and then ripped the shredded pieces into even smaller torn threads.

Hannah's tears wounded her mother. Rachel felt an awful pain in her head and belly and decided she had to do something. Somehow her Dovid had become overrun with some darkness.

She first discreetly approached the wives of Dovid's employees. Were their husbands working late each night at the grain silos? Had they heard that the business was taking up so much time?

No, Rachel was told, their husbands were home at dinner, same as always. They had no idea what she was speaking about.

Determined to solve the strange riddle of her husband's erratic behavior, Rachel spied one night on her husband. After Dovid had left and the children had gone to sleep, she walked to the grain silo. She slowly opened the door and saw a dim yellow candlelight, but her husband was not there.

Sounds arose from a corner. Rachel thought there were animals hissing and fighting with each other, perhaps eating her husband's grain. She walked in the direction of the sounds, intending, if nothing else, to shoo the rodents away.

Rachel's eyes became slightly accustomed to the blackness, but she still could not see well. She groped in front of her, trying to find a way through the maze of grain sacks. She followed the animal sounds and felt encouraged as they grew louder.

Then Rachel saw it: Her husband was naked and moaning, his eyes glazed over and turned completely white. He was embracing and kissing a creature with long, flat, blonde hair, but reddish, speckled skin, chicken legs, and two horns sprouting from its head.

Rachel screamed. Dovid remained oblivious in his trance. The creature slowly looked up at Rachel; the creature had Maryska's face. It laughed at her and returned to kissing Dovid.

Rachel ran outside. The sky was thick with dark clouds, and the stars were not visible. She could not focus her thoughts and stumbled around looking for some light in the black night. Finally, she saw the light of the *Bet Midrash,* which was never put out.

Rachel barged into the *Bet Midrash,* seeking the reassurance of a lighted room. There were a couple of men sprawled on the benches and snoring. The half-asleep beadle saw her and muttered something inaudible.

In the corner was an old man swaying over a text. He was tall and thin, with an unkempt, tangled white beard, which hung down past his chin and clothes splattered with dried mud. The old man had remarkable energy, however, as he swayed and studied with wild enthusiasm, even after his fellow scholars had fallen asleep.

Rachel stared at the man for some time. The sound of his voice reciting the text—she had no idea what it was; she only knew Yiddish, and this was not Yiddish. She thought it must have been something in Hebrew or Aramaic—it soothed her nerves and made her hopeful, although she did not know why.

The man eventually turned away from his book and looked up at her. He smiled at Rachel and she thought he seemed to recognize her, although she had never met him before:

Good, you are here. I have been waiting for you. I am here to help you. Your troubles drew me here.

The man said his name was Eliyahu. He claimed to be a kabbalist who traveled from town to town using his esoteric learning to assist his fellow Jews—an amulet for a sick child, or a special combination of holy names to soften the heart of a cruel Polish lord. Eliyahu said he had no fixed residence, but always managed to turn up a crust of bread and a little cup of wine to welcome the *Shabbat* Queen on Friday evenings.

Three nights ago, Eliyahu continued, he was on a road near this town. He had felt tired from walking and stopped for a nap.

Then Eliyahu had a vivid dream: He saw a demon, a daughter of the demon queen, Lilith, who had long blonde hair falling over and behind her horns. This demon, whose true name he knew, but dared not utter, was kissing a Jewish man. Eliyahu called out to her to stop, but she only cackled and hissed. The man seemed unable to hear. The demon's kiss was loud, with alternating smacking and slurping sounds. The sounds grew louder as Eliyahu watched the couple in his dream, and his head pounded in pain. The demon's lips appeared to grow larger, until they were the lips of a freakish giant, easily able to swallow her now much smaller human lover. The large demon lips parted, and a green tongue with a snake's head came out and wrapped itself around the besotted fool.

At this point Eliyahu had awoken and noticed his breathing was labored. He was certain this was no idle dream, but rather, he had been gifted with a vision by the Holy One, Blessed be He, so that Eliyahu could save the ensnared man before it was too late.

Eliyahu had walked to an inn close by where he could expect free room and board, as he had saved the innkeeper's young son from a terrible illness one winter. Once inside and warmed with a glass of tea, Eliyahu prayed with special combinations of the letters of one of the names of the Holy One, Blessed be He, for an answer in his next dream to the riddle of the terrifying vision of the demon kiss.

In his dream that night, Eliyahu had felt himself ascending to the upper worlds, where he met King Solomon, who revealed that the demon Eliyahu had seen had indeed sunk her claws into a Jewish householder in the town where Rachel lived. Solomon advised him to go to the *Bet Midrash* of the town, purify himself through prayers and fasting, and await the man's wife.

And now here you are, good lady. Tell me, did you see anything strange tonight?

Rachel looked at the ground. Her head hurt; she stumbled and collapsed upon a bench opposite Eliyahu. She was silent for a brief time and then sobbed softly.

What did you see?

Rachel could not answer. She held her head, which felt as if it were being pelted with rocks, and gave out muffled, tearful moans.

Eliyahu repeated his question, more firmly this time:

What did you see? I cannot help if you do not speak.

With effort, Rachel calmed her rapid breathing. She spoke of what she had seen in the grain silo between her husband and a not human creature that resembled her maid, Maryska. More than once Rachel interrupted her story to let out a new wave of tears.

Rabbi, now you know what I saw. What can I do? How could this happen to my Dovid?

Eliyahu sighed. He mumbled a prayer quickly; Rachel could not understand him, but trusted he was somehow going to save her and Dovid from whatever thing was Maryska.

Eliyahu reached down to the floor and pulled a satchel up to the top of the table between the bench where he sat and the bench where Rachel sat. He absentmindedly hummed a melody while rummaging through the bag's contents. Rachel saw all sorts of odds and ends emerge onto the table: books thick and thin, all clearly worn from heavy use, a variety of different amulets, and innumerable scraps of paper covered in tiny, meandering Hebrew script.

Yes, here, this is it.

Eliyahu held up a particular amulet, a flat green disc, which Rachel could see opened on the left side. This disc was connected to a simple necklace.

Eliyahu turned his eyes back to Rachel:

When your husband is home again, you must place this amulet around his neck. Inside is a special combination of the letters of a hidden name of the Holy One, Blessed be He, and the letters of the true name of the demon that has taken your maid's form as an earthly husk. Once this amulet is around his neck, your husband will be free from her power, and his lusts—which the she-demon has carefully stoked like a well-tended fire—will die down. He will be returned to you.

But you must act quickly. The demon saw you. She will take action against you soon. I do not know how, but she will do you grave harm. You are a threat now to whatever she wishes to do.

Now go, see if your Dovid is back in his bed. Perhaps you shall be able to place this amulet upon his neck tonight.

Rachel took the amulet, thanked Eliyahu in a choked voice, and hurried home.

Rachel crept into the house. As she passed Maryska's cot, she heard her maid snoring loudly and saw a grin on her sleeping face. Saliva was dribbling out of the side of her mouth. Rachel thought Maryska resembled a wild, snorting boar sleeping in the forest.

Upstairs she found her Dovid sleeping in his bed. Rachel had always remembered Dovid as an agitated sleeper: He tossed and turned, his arms and legs flailed about, and more than once he woke up entangled in his blankets like they were woolen spider webs.

He looked so different now, lying stiffly on his back. Yet Rachel thought he did not look peaceful. He seemed lifeless and shriveled, like a dried up raisin. Dovid did not snore. He just barely breathed.

Rachel leaned over his face. She had planned to place the amulet around his neck, but she now hesitated. Looking at him Rachel saw again, in her mind, Dovid feasting hungrily upon that vile horned creature's lips, and she was filled with hatred. It would serve him right, she thought, to be eaten up by this creature. He was neither husband nor father any more. Maybe the creature would use up his disgusting, lecherous soul and leave Rachel to live out her days as a widow—that would be better than seeing Dovid each day, better than looking at those lips glazed with Maryska's saliva.

And Rachel need not remain an unmarried widow. She was still, she hoped, an attractive woman—three quick spits on the ground to ward off the evil eye—and had a large dowry. No doubt a pious, wealthy widower would take her as a wife.

But then she thought of her children. What if Maryska took her time with Dovid? That could be years of torment for the children. Rachel thought of how Dovid had hurt poor little Hannah and shuddered.

Or what if Maryska impoverished them? She could steal their money. Or convince Dovid to waste it in some foolish scheme. Who knew the limits of the demon's mischief? Without money, Nachman's education would end, and he would not become a scholar. None of the girls, who needed dowries, would marry well. The family would sink into the mud. Rachel saw herself, in rags, selling rotted apples in the marketplace. She pictured herself begging a filthy, unlearned blacksmith to marry his son to her Hannah.

So she decided she must do the deed. Not, Rachel told herself, for Dovid, may his name be cursed and blotted out, but for the children. Thus, she rested the amulet on Dovid's chest and gently pulled the necklace over his head. She lifted his limp head up and pulled the necklace down the back of his throat. Dovid remained inert. Rachel reflected that she could have strangled Dovid with the necklace if she had wanted to.

Rachel slept fitfully for what little remained of the night. At sunrise she woke with a sudden jolt of restlessness. Wondering if the previous night's adventures had been a crazy dream, she walked over to Dovid's bed, but the sight of the amulet on his still barely breathing body forced her to admit it had all actually happened.

Rachel decided to test the amulet. She went downstairs and woke Maryska and told her the master was awake and wanted tea. Maryska lumbered out of her bed and brewed a pot of tea. When it was ready, she placed a glass of tea and the box of sugar cubes on a small tray and went upstairs.

Rachel heard a door creak open and then the sounds of broken pieces of glass. Maryska ran back downstairs; her face was pale and she was vomiting. Maryska did not look at Rachel, but bolted away with an agile swiftness which Rachel had never imagined possible for Maryska's lazy bovine body.

Rachel went upstairs again to Dovid's bed. The tray and box of sugar were on the ground. The glass of tea had shattered, spilling its contents on the floor. There were streaks of green vomit on the floor and on Dovid's blankets, but not on him. Dovid continued to sleep, as if he were still in the cradle of a quiet midnight.

Rachel went downstairs to grab a mop to clean up Maryska's mess. There was no longer any sign of Maryska in the house. Hannah awoke and asked what was wrong—she had heard screaming and running. Rachel told her Maryska was sick and was going away, and the two of them needed to clean up papa's room.

After cleaning up, Rachel strode giddily to the *Bet Midrash* eager to thank Eliyahu and to offer payment for his services. But Rachel did not see him when she entered. The building was empty save for the sleeping beadle; Rachel poked him with her walking stick.

Where is Eliyahu, the kabbalist, who came last night? The stranger? I must see him.

The beadle rubbed his eyes:

What stranger? No strangers have come here.

Last night, I saw him. He said his name was Eliyahu. He was here in this place, and I spoke to him. You were all asleep but he was awake and studying the holy texts and we spoke. Where is he?

I saw no one.

The beadle went back to sleep. Rachel searched all over town, but could find no trace of Eliyahu as no one else had seen or met him. Rachel finally concluded that Eliyahu must have been Eliyahu HaNavi, Elijah the Prophet, sent down from Paradise to help her, a Jewish mother in need. She smiled to herself and thanked the Holy One, Blessed be He.

Dovid slept most of the day. When he woke, his limbs were stiff and his temples pounded. He pulled himself up in bed, but fell over when he tried to stand. Sitting on the floor by the bed, Dovid's mind cleared, and he saw a vision of Maryska as Rachel had seen her: with horns and chicken legs and hideous scaly skin. Dovid shuddered. He knew he had been a pathetic fool and a terrible husband. He saw Rachel's face in his mind and sobbed loudly. Dovid felt an urge to hurt himself; he clenched his right hand into a tight fist and hit himself repeatedly on the forehead. His stomach knotted in pain and he felt nauseous, although he did not vomit.

Dovid eventually stopped crying and was able to stand up. He felt the amulet hanging around his neck. Dovid was unsure where it had come from, but he deduced that the amulet must have broken the demon's power of illusion. He dared not remove it. Dovid mumbled a prayer of gratitude to the Holy One, Blessed be He, for this miracle.

Dovid swore he would be a good husband from that point forward. He resolved to dismiss Maryska then and there from his household service. He imagined himself sending Maryska off in various ways: in rage, in cold politeness, in apology. Yet in several of these daydreams Maryska tossed her hair and touched Dovid's arm, convincing him to reconsider. So Dovid was relieved to learn Maryska had departed of her own accord. He did not ask after the details.

Dovid now tried his best to make Rachel happy. He surprised her by bringing in the best tailor in town to make a set of new dresses. He praised, loudly and frequently, Rachel's good sense, fine housekeeping, and pious character. Dovid insisted to the children that they should be grateful for having such a wonderful mother, and he flew into a rage if a child argued that Rachel was mean or unfair.

Rachel was not entirely comfortable with her husband's intense adoration. Something about his mad insistence upon her perfect goodness made Rachel uneasy in her skin. She did not encourage Dovid, but instead smiled awkwardly at the ground and told him to think about more important matters than her.

However, one legacy of Maryska stuck: Dovid's dishonest business practices. Given how much Maryska had demanded and taken, Dovid lacked the resources to pay back all the money he had appropriated by fraud. Well, he thought, no one has complained yet, so my little tricks must not be that important. I will continue until I have rebuilt my savings—Hannah will need a dowry, and Nachman will no doubt demand new and better books and tutors—and then gradually return to honest ways of doing business.

But Dovid never could bring himself to forego the extra income, and he always had a reason to delay remedying his conduct—the money was needed for the children, or Rachel, or to repair his wagon, or for a new horse; there was always something. So the years passed and Dovid grew accustomed to dishonesty as a way of doing business. Everyone skims a little extra, Dovid would tell himself.

Several months passed after Maryska's departure. Dovid continued to wear his amulet, even when he bathed, as he was convinced he would fall back under Maryska's evil spell if he took it off. Nevertheless, Dovid worried the demon's kisses may have planted something unholy in his body. He imagined black-eyed maggots crawling around the inside of his flesh and feasting upon his innards. Every pain in his belly caused Dovid to break into a sweat and, heart racing, dash to a secluded corner. With tears streaming down, Dovid would pray to the Holy One, Blessed be He, to save him.

Dovid never asked Rachel, or anyone else, where the amulet had come from. He chose to believe his dead parents had sent a kindly angel to save him. Dovid was sure that whoever gave the amulet to him possessed knowledge of matters normally hidden from a mortal man's limited perception. But his parents in the other world, the world to come, no doubt saw his sufferings and sins and reached out to redeem his depraved soul. His true parents were always watching over him, Dovid thought.

One sleepy, humid afternoon Moshe returned to Dovid's town. He invited Dovid to his room at the local inn and poured out two small glasses of brandy. After swirling, sniffing, and sampling the brandy, Moshe leaned over and asked Dovid with a smile:

So, did you take my advice? Was the maid all I promised she would be? Don't be shy—it is just you and me.

To my great shame, Dovid replied, I lay with her. She was a demon and I was only saved, just barely, by this amulet brought to me from Paradise by an angel.

Dovid pulled the amulet out from under his shirt so Moshe could see it. He did not take it off.

Demons and angels and Paradise? Have you lost your mind? Why should a demon or an angel want anything to do with you? What happened? Did you have your fun or not?

So Dovid told Moshe the story of his affair with Maryska.

And now, Dovid concluded, if I remove the amulet, the maggots will eat me alive. Or Maryska will return to finish devouring my soul.

You idiot. Maryska left because she had cadged enough money and grew tired of you. Your crazy sleep was no doubt because she drugged you to have enough time to complete her escape. She and her Ivan are no doubt drinking your money away in a tavern somewhere. You want to know, great mystical sage, where that amulet came from? The thieving whore put it around your neck so your head would fill with silly mumbo-jumbo instead of the simple truth.

Moshe laughed and took another drink of brandy. Dovid looked at his feet. Moshe's words had stung. Perhaps he was being a silly fool. Wasn't it a simpler explanation that the greedy girl had made off with the money once she had enough? It was a little crazy to imagine he was in some grand struggle with supernatural beings as opposed to the everyday sordidness of adultery with a greedy servant.

Moshe put his glass down, yawned, and smiled broadly. I will show you how ridiculous you are, he said. And with a quick cat-like sweep of his hand, Moshe grabbed the amulet and tore it from Dovid's neck.

Do you see any demons materializing in this room? Are the maggots eating your flesh?

Moshe laughed. Dovid, consumed with shame, was silent. Moshe started tossing the amulet up in the air and catching it, like it was a small ball. Then suddenly Moshe hurled the amulet hard against the wall. It shattered into tiny pieces.

The whore did not even invest in a well-made fake. You thought that flimsy thing was going to battle demons? Let's talk about something more serious. Tell me again, how is Nachman's education coming? Can we go over and test him? I want to be sure you have kept your promise to me and you are minding the boy's education.

VI. The Penitent

IT HAD NOW been many weeks since Dovid and Rachel had received any news from Nachman. This was despite the fact that, by any reasonable reckoning, Nachman and Moshe should have long ago arrived at Moshe's town in White Russia.

There was little conversation in the house. Dovid ate and dressed quickly and busied himself with work. He would not speak of Nachman, but when Dovid passed the library room where Nachman had studied all those years, he would sometimes hesitate, peek in, and then hurry away with his eyes on the ground.

Rachel's worries mounted. She took to praying frequently with her woman's Yiddish prayer book, both in the women's section of the synagogue and at home. She forced herself to fast, so her sins would be forgiven and the Throne of Glory in Paradise would receive her supplications. She would squelch her desire to speak—after all, what good would her chatter do? But sometimes she could not bear it any longer:

Do you think Nachman is safe? Perhaps robbers attacked them on the road? Maybe robbers live in that abandoned ruin Moshe wanted to inspect? Or did Nachman fall ill, so ill that he cannot write? Or maybe he rejected the bride and Moshe has done something terrible in retribution? There must be a reason why our Nachman is silent, right, isn't that true? There must be?

Dovid would not look at Rachel. He stared straight ahead, at a wall, and sighed. It did not help that Rachel's pent up anxiety had a tendency to spill out late at night, after she had spent herself in prayer, when Dovid was exhausted from the day's labors.

His eyes fixed on the wall, Dovid responded to these questions with a façade of calm: Moshe is a good man. Be patient, I am sure everything is fine. You'll see. Tomorrow, or the next day, a letter will come and you will be ashamed of how silly you are being.

But with each passing day Dovid's voice grew shakier, although also louder and more insistent. Dovid began to interrupt Rachel before she could finish her litany of questions. If Rachel tried to continue, Dovid erupted:

What is wrong with you? Do you think I would send my only son, the child who will say *Kaddish* for my soul one day, off to be harmed? Everything will turn out for the best, and you will wallow in shame for your ridiculous outbursts.

Dovid would then sit perfectly still and ignore any further words from Rachel. Sometimes she gave up quickly; sometimes she continued to berate her husband for some time. And sometimes she sobbed. Dovid betrayed no reaction.

Rachel eventually decided she must take some action to help her Nachman. She considered hiring a coach and driver, but she did not know Nachman's exact whereabouts. So she reasoned she should first find a way to determine Nachman's location.

There was a woman, a Ukrainian Christian, who lived on the outskirts of town, and who was well known for her special knowledge of things hidden. She had a reputation among the Christians in the region—including the gentry—as a healer and as a witch. Some Jews of the town, too, found their way to the Christian good witch and sought her aid. However, when the rabbi and the town's leading Jewish householders discovered Jews were availing themselves of this black magic, they forbade any Jew to visit the woman.

In happier days Rachel had heartily approved of this decree and loudly championed it among the town's Jewish women. But Rachel now regretted her arrogant disdain for the Christian wonder-worker. Desperate for news of Nachman, but ashamed to confide in a fellow Jew (for what would she think of a Jewish mother who sent her son off on such a crazy journey?), Rachel decided to visit the Christian witch.

After dinner one night, Rachel said she had left something at the tailor's workshop, which she needed to pick up. She told Hannah to make sure the younger children were put to bed, grabbed her purse, and left the house. Dovid paid no attention.

Rachel avoided the main streets of the town, instead snaking behind the town's houses and in and out of the abutting farmlands. By this roundabout route, she slowly arrived at the southern edge of the town, where there was a forest. Rachel followed a narrow and somewhat overgrown footpath into the woods. Although the moon shone brightly, its rays were blocked by the thick branches, and Rachel could barely see where the path led. She tripped at one point, on a large, jagged rock, but was able to get back up again by grabbing the tree branches for support.

Rachel reached a wide clearing with a peasant's one-room hut in the center. There was smoke rising from the chimney and the sound of pots banging. Rachel approached the hut and knocked gently.

Who is there? Don't you know it is late? Come back in the morning.

Dear Mother, I need your help, but I cannot come in the daylight. I am a Jewish woman, my name is Rachel. You know it is forbidden for me to knock on your door. So I can only come when I am hidden by the darkness.

If it is forbidden for you to be here, then go away and leave me in peace. I am old, I need my rest.

Please, Mother, don't turn me away. I need your help. My boy, the apple of my eye, has disappeared and I need your help to find him. I have money with me.

There was a pause. Rachel tried to calm her racing pulse, but without much success.

Fine, come in.

Rachel pushed the door open and walked in. The cold night breeze made the fire flicker. The ceiling of the hut was low, and Rachel had to stoop slightly. The hut was one big room with an earthen floor and walls stained with soot. A girl whom Rachel guessed was ten years old or so tended the fire and was cooking something in a pot.

Near the fire sat a squat old woman wrapped in damp, filthy rags. The old woman wore a kerchief, but Rachel could tell that her head underneath had only sparse wisps of white hair. The old woman had thick eyebrows and a wide mouth flanked by folds of wrinkles. The old woman turned towards Rachel.

You are a fine lady. So, you are here. What can I do for you?

Rachel smoothed her dress and inhaled deeply:

Thank you, kind Mother, for seeing me. My only son, my Nachman, was to be betrothed to a girl in White Russia. He left with his prospective father-in-law to meet the bride. It is weeks since we have heard from them. I am so scared. I keep imagining the worst. I have to know where my Nachman is and if he is safe. Can you help me?

The old woman nodded and shouted to the young girl by the fire to bring over what she needed. The girl left the fire and brought a bowl and several little bottles to the old woman's lap.

The old woman motioned for Rachel to sit down next to her on the floor. The old woman poured different liquids into the bowl and mixed them with her finger. She mumbled some incantations. She asked again the name of Rachel's son and intoned the name Nachman in a loud, booming tone.

The old woman finished and then stared into the bowl for some time. After what seemed to Rachel to be an unbearably long wait, the old woman put the bowl on the ground and cursed it.

I cannot summon an image of your son. The spell failed.

What does that mean, Mother? Why can't you see my Nachman?

I am being blocked. Something not human is involved. Even a human sorcerer or witch could not block my spell this completely. There is something beyond my power involved.

Rachel thanked the old witch and paid her. On the walk home, Rachel became convinced that Maryska, that demon, had found her Nachman and done some terrible deed in revenge for Rachel's driving her away all those years ago. Rachel knew she needed a scholar learned in esoteric lore to fight the demon, but she could not think of who could help.

Rachel did not tell her husband, or anyone else, what had transpired that evening. In the following days, she locked herself in her room and prayed without stop. She begged the Holy One, Blessed be He, to send her help. She thought she needed Eliyahu HaNavi to return, but decided it would be too presumptuous for her to request that such an important personage in the upper worlds be sent to address her petty problems.

After hours of fasting and praying, Rachel would leave her house to run the errands typical of every Jewish housewife. In the marketplace, her head throbbed and she was always dizzy and exhausted. If the wind was blowing, it lashed her skin bitterly; if the sun shined, then the light was painful to her eyes, which now preferred the dark.

She no longer could gossip with her friends; their worries—about lazy maids, overpriced kosher meat, or the terrible decline in the quality of the *cheder*—struck Rachel as hopelessly beside the point. Even more maddening to her, Rachel's friends never asked after her Nachman, but rather appeared to assume he must be just fine wherever he had gone. They did ask after Hannah and her betrothal plans, but this also struck Rachel as absurd: Hannah is here, she thought, and not leaving—so why the fuss? She will marry when she will marry, but Nachman is in the hands of a demon.

Rachel thought of seeking help from the *rebbetzin*, the wife of the rabbi of the Great Synagogue and a shrewd and learned woman. But to ask for help, Rachel would have to explain the entire shameful story of her husband's seduction by a demon and his filthy adultery. Rachel did not want to discuss these things aloud and never had. And what about the shame she would bring on her family? Once she told one person, who could tell where such a story would travel?

One Saturday morning, in the Great Synagogue, Rachel was praying fervently in the women's section, which was located in a balcony above the main sanctuary. By this time Rachel had become gaunt and drawn, and her eyes were stained red from heavy weeping. She prayed by herself in the corner; her puffy eyes glaring into the unseen distance disturbed Rachel's fellow housewives and made them shy away.

Rachel looked up towards the curtain covering the front of the women's section, which was slightly ajar. Through a slit Rachel could see him sitting and praying below—she could see Eliyahu HaNavi, just as he had looked years ago on that dark night in the *Bet Midrash*. She audibly gasped for joy and grinned madly, bearing her now blackened teeth. The other women looked at Rachel. This bizarre outburst settled them in their conviction that Rachel had somehow lost her mind.

Rachel did not care about their dirty, furtive looks. She kissed her Yiddish prayer book and hurried downstairs. While she could not enter the men's sanctuary, she positioned herself outside the doors of the Great Synagogue and waited for the men to leave.

Eventually the men trickled out, sometimes in little groups with animated conversations and sometimes alone. Rachel waited and watched. More groups of men came out. Dovid walked out by himself, humming a soft melody and staring into the distance. He did not notice his wife standing nearby.

Still, there was no Eliyahu HaNavi. Once Rachel was certain all of the men must have gone home, she walked into the vestibule and peeked into the main sanctuary. Perhaps, she told herself, Eliyahu HaNavi will be waiting there for me again. But she saw no one inside.

Rachel slunk back to her house and lay down on a couch. She decided she must be losing her wits. She closed her eyes, but her sleep troubled her. In her dreams she saw Eliyahu HaNavi everywhere in town: in the Great Synagogue, in the *Bet Midrash*, in the marketplace, standing by the *cheder*, on the road leading out of town, even in the witch's hut.

Over the next several days, Rachel's dream came true: Eliyahu HaNavi was everywhere. She saw him out her window, in the marketplace, and everywhere else she looked. Yet she saw him only in fleeting images—a profile looking away from her and then disappearing around the next corner. When Rachel tried to follow him, he vanished. Rachel asked around about a visitor to town, an elderly man who studied the kabbalah. No one, however, had seen any newcomer who fit Rachel's description.

Rachel could not take this teasing. Had her prayers been answered? Had the Holy One, Blessed be He, sent His prophet Eliyahu from Paradise to Earth to help her rescue Nachman? Or was this another demon trick, a practical joke played by a malicious, tiny cackling imp to drive Rachel into madness?

Rachel could not sleep. She woke in a sweat and opened a window. The half-moon and mass of stars shone brightly in the cloudless sky. It was quite late; she could hear Dovid's croaking snores. On a whim, Rachel got up from bed, threw a shawl and coat over her nightgown, laced up her boots, and went for a walk.

Once again, the only light below the sky was from the *Bet Midrash*. Rachel walked towards it feeling guided by some unseen force. She pulled the door open and walked inside.

The interior was empty, except for one or two men lying on benches, fast asleep, and one old man swaying in the corner over a holy book and chanting softly in Hebrew, which Rachel could not understand. Rachel walked up to the old man, slowly and gingerly, so as not to disturb him. The man's back was facing her, and he seemed not to notice Rachel's presence.

The old man's chanting ceased. He turned around on his bench, looked up at Rachel, and flashed a friendly smile.

Rachel was flooded with joy—it was him, really him, standing right before her in the same place she had last seen him.

Is it you? She whispered.

Yes, I am here. Have you come about Nachman? Your prayers have ascended to the Throne of Glory in Paradise and the Holy One, Blessed be He, has sent me to you.

Where is my Nachman? Is he safe?

Nachman is in terrible danger. The creature whom you know as Moshe is no man, but a hideous demon who has haunted and tempted your husband for many years. I dare not utter Moshe's true name in the demon tongue. But he plans to make your Nachman a servant of Ashmedai, king of demons, and the legions of *Gehenna*. However, because Moshe's strength comes from Dovid's sins, you cannot save your son. Only Dovid can. You must tell your husband to come here, tomorrow night, after the towns-people have fallen asleep. I am not permitted to say more to you.

Rachel's joy faded, and she pulsated with hate for her husband. Not only had the disgusting lecher betrayed her with a demon whore, but now he had sold their only son, their *Kaddish*, to a second demon. She cursed her father for marrying her to this sinning fool. Rachel stood for some time lost in her bitter thoughts.

You must go, you need your rest. There is no more you can do tonight.

Rachel silently obeyed and walked home. She did not lie back down in her own bed, but walked over to the sleeping Dovid. He had a smug grin on his face; his dreams appeared happy. His toes twitched with what Rachel was sure was delight at some disgusting fantasy.

Rachel thought: You killed him. You murdered my Nachman, my *Kaddish*. She saw him again, in the grain silo, coiled with the demon. Rachel saw a pillow lying nearby and imagined herself smothering Dovid. She could live out her days as a pious widow and marry her girls off to excellent bridegrooms. Or, given her sizeable dowry, she could remarry and this time, pick the man herself. She would choose an elderly scholar, a widower, whom she would care for and who would teach her the wisdom of the holy sages.

But Rachel stopped herself. Much as she hated Dovid, he was the only hope of saving Nachman. She willed herself to suppress her hate for Nachman's sake. She would speak to Dovid tomorrow, after she had a chance to rest and calm her nerves.

Rachel did not wake until well into the morning, after Dovid had already left. All day Rachel practiced her approach to Dovid. Unfortunately, in many of these daydreams, Rachel's kind, calculated words morphed into angry reproaches and accusations of murder and adultery. Rachel told herself repeatedly: She must be kind to Dovid, Nachman needed his mother to be strong now, but her hatred kept bubbling up.

Dovid returned home for dinner. He seemed the same as ever to his wife: He ate with gusto (especially the pickled herring), and commented about how business was looking up, and how Count So and So's agent had paid an unexpected visit—real potential there. He struck Rachel as unconcerned with Nachman's peril—and he had caused it all! Her eyes narrowed with rage, but she checked herself. She must trust in Eliyahu HaNavi and the Holy One, Blessed be He.

After Dovid recited the grace after meals, Rachel asked to have a word with him privately. She led Dovid into Nachman's abandoned study on the first floor, lit a candle, and closed the door. There was a thick cloud of dust in the room. Rachel stood by the lectern; Dovid sat down on a stool. He shook his leg and twitched uncomfortably.

Rachel took a deep breath and spoke in a clear, steady voice:

We need to discuss Nachman. We have not heard from him or Moshe in months. Something is wrong. You know this, too, if you will only permit yourself to think about it. I have prayed to the Holy One, Blessed be He, for guidance. Last night He woke me and guided me to the *Bet Midrash*. There was one man awake there, an old humble stranger, swaying over a holy book. I somehow knew I must approach this man.

The old man turned to face me. He had such kind eyes. Those eyes would melt your soul. He asked me if I had come to seek help for Nachman. I had said nothing, and he is a stranger, so I asked how he could know who my Nachman was? Was he a sorcerer?

He laughed. He told me my prayers had reached the Throne of Glory, and that the Holy One, Blessed be He, had chosen to send him, Eliyahu HaNavi, to help us. He told me Nachman is in terrible danger, but he needed to speak to you to help him. Eliyahu

HaNavi left me with the message that you must go to him tonight, after midnight, in the *Bet Midrash*. So you must go. Promise me you will go.

Dovid had not looked at Rachel during this speech. His eyes instead darted rapidly around the spines and covers of the various books in the room. He had tried to make out the titles, but his Hebrew was too poor.

Dovid did not reply. Rachel noticed he was not looking at her, and she felt anger stirring in her chest. Calm down, she told herself, angry words will only drive him away. She willed her voice into a sweet tone:

Please, Dovid, for the sake of our Nachman, promise me you will see Eliyahu HaNavi tonight.

Dovid looked up at Rachel:

Are you crazy? You met some lunatic in the *Bet Midrash*—and what you were doing there in the middle of the night is beyond me—and you think you spoke to an emissary from the Throne of Glory? I am sure Nachman is fine and is probably lost in some *Bet Midrash* in White Russia debating the fine points of the Torah. Or maybe he is learning Moshe's business. What terrible danger could he be in? An excess of *kugel*?

Rachel could no longer contain herself:

How can you condemn our Nachman to his suffering so cruelly? Eliyahu HaNavi told me he has fallen into the clutches of demons. Demons! Who knows what horrible torments he has already endured? *Nu*, you think I am crazy, but just go see him tonight. As a favor to me in recognition of my long years toiling as your wife. If you still think Eliyahu HaNavi is merely another beggar, then I will not bother you again. But promise me, please, you will see him tonight.

Dovid looked down and sighed. Rachel's mention of their many long years of marriage reminded him of how he had betrayed her with Maryska. Would it be so terrible for him to indulge her? He can make small talk with the smelly beggar tonight and soothe Rachel's nerves.

Fine, I will go.

Rachel smiled and clasped her hands. They spoke no more, and quickly exited Nachman's study.

Dovid fell asleep at his normal time, and groaned his typical loud snores. Rachel stayed awake near his bed, praying fervently and begging the Holy One, Blessed be He, to pardon Dovid's sins and to deliver her son back to her arms.

When it was just past midnight, Rachel shook Dovid violently. He took a few moments to wake, and even then his head was heavy with the fog of sleepiness. Rachel pulled his blankets off and dressed him herself, like he was a small boy again.

Rachel led Dovid to the door and pushed him outside. The night was chilly, and the cold air made Dovid more alert. He took a moment to get his bearings and remembered his errand—to the *Bet Midrash* and the smelly beggar.

The *Bet Midrash* was easy to find at night, as it was one of the few buildings giving off any light in the darkness. Nevertheless, Dovid's tired limbs were clumsy; he tripped once or twice and found it hard to steady himself. Sleepiness is like drunkenness, Dovid thought.

Dovid arrived at the door to the *Bet Midrash*. His pant leg was ripped and blood-stained, from where he had tripped on the way, and the scrape on his knee stung. Dovid cursed Rachel for her mad superstition and could not understand why he was making a fool of himself because of some mad beggar. He thought briefly of simply returning home, but the night breeze chilled his bones, and he wanted to warm himself inside the *Bet Midrash*. He assumed he would walk in, find no one, warm up a bit, and get back to his bed.

Dovid gently pushed the door open. Inside he saw a couple of young students sleeping on benches. Despite the fact that their bodies were emaciated from lack of food, these skeletal dreamers smiled sweetly in their sleep. Dovid thought they seemed happy enough to have a roof over their heads, and their beloved holy books on nearby tables. And they were far away from nagging wives, if they even had any.

Dovid suddenly became aware of a murmuring in the far right corner of the room. The chant was faint, but Dovid could tell it was Hebrew and that there was a steady rhythm. Dovid craned his neck in the direction of the chanting. He saw a tall, gaunt old man bent over a thick book. The man's head seemed practically to disappear into the book. Dovid thought this man must be quite near sighted.

Dovid found himself hypnotized by the melancholy chanting. Without realizing it, his body pivoted in the direction of the old man and Dovid took a couple of steps towards him. Dovid could not tell if he was awake or dreaming. His head felt heavy and he seemed to see the world through a sleepy fog in which everything was blurred except the sad but sweet Hebrew chanting.

The old man stopped. He sat upright and turned around, but without getting up from his bench. He looked at Dovid and smiled. In a loud voice, he called out:

Reb Dovid, it is good to see you on such a fine night. Come sit with me.

Dovid was startled out of his drowsiness. He looked back at the two sleeping youths; he could not understand why the old man's yelling had not woken either of them. Dovid was surprised, too, that the old man knew his name, but figured Rachel must have told him.

Dovid decided he may as well play along, if only to humor Rachel, and walked over. The old man had, in the meantime, pulled a large round of hard yellow cheese and a small knife from his satchel. He recited the blessing, cut himself a piece, and then chewed merrily.

Would you like some, Reb Dovid? The cheese is good. It was a parting gift in the town of Berdichev from a wealthy householder. The man, may his name be blessed, gave me food and shelter for the holy *Shabbat*, and then gave me a fine cheese for the road. There are not enough like him in the world.

Dovid said nothing. How could Dovid tell this insomniac beggar that his wife had somehow deluded herself into believing him to be Eliyahu HaNavi, descended from Paradise to rescue Nachman? So Dovid simply stared at the old man.

The old man ate several more pieces of cheese. He hummed, quite loudly, but somehow did not wake the sleeping young men. Eventually the old man returned the cheese and knife to his satchel, let out a sound that mixed a deep sigh and a burp, and addressed himself to Dovid:

I see, Reb Dovid, you are not one for idle chatter. Good for you. There is too much idle chatter in this world. I will get right to the point. I am Eliyahu HaNavi, and I have come down to Earth from the higher realms to help rescue your Nachman, whose wisdom and purity have not gone unnoticed in the World to Come. Nachman has fallen into the clutches of demons, and if you do not repent your horrible sins, truly repent and give up the worldly goods for which you have traded your son's soul, then both you and Nachman shall be lost.

Dovid looked on impassively through the old man's speech, but at the end he could no longer contain his laughter. This is ridiculous, Dovid thought.

The old man's face hardened. In one swift stroke he smacked Dovid's laughing cheek with a strength Dovid did not imagine could be contained in such a weak, old frame. Dovid stopped laughing.

You disgusting fool. You laugh at the emissary from the Throne of Glory? I can see your soul, rotted and putrid. It will be scraps for the dogs of *Gehenna*. It would be fitting to let you stew in your own filth, but I have not been sent on your account. I am here because of the many merits of Nachman, a true saint, and you, unfortunately, are the one whose help is necessary to save that saint.

You still don't believe that I am who I say I am? I know you have sinned with that disgusting she-demon who called herself Maryska. And I know you cheat in your business dealings. Your weights and measures are false, and you have stolen, again and again, from Jew and Gentile alike.

Did you ever wonder why you were such easy prey for Maryska? Are you still foolish enough to blame your wife Rachel, a good pious woman, for not caving into your sick lusts?

Your soul was already shriveled when you fell into Maryska's hands. You had sold your child to a demon for earthly riches, and by that foul deed you lost your portion in the World to Come and became a plaything for the evil spirits who creep hungrily through the world.

Why do you look puzzled? Your friend Moshe gave you a deal: When the time was right, you were to deliver your son up to him. In exchange, Moshe would make you wealthy. And you said yes!

Now you have fulfilled your bargain with your friend Moshe. You do realize that this man whom you call Moshe—and you cannot imagine how this infuriates the true *Moshe Rabbenu* in Paradise—is in fact a demon? You sold your child to a demon so you can eat succulent goose meat each night of the week and have a fat belly.

Still, Nachman is a good soul and his weeping reached the
Throne of Glory. A heavenly decree was issued to spare him. The
angel Metatron was readying himself for the task when Ashmedai,
king of the demons, approached the Throne of Glory to object.
Ashmedai pointed out there was a valid contract between himself
and you, Reb Dovid. Ashmedai said the demon realm had fulfilled
its part of the contract and delivered unto you the promised benefit
of worldly wealth. It is not proper, Ashmedai argued, for the demons to lose Nachman's soul if you were to retain the benefits of
the contract.

There was much debate at the heavenly court. The angels
could not settle the matter themselves, so they consulted with
the greatest sages in the Celestial Academy, with *Moshe Rabbenu*,
and King Solomon, and Akiba, and Shimon bar Yochai. After
much back and forth, and arguing and counter-arguing, the
decision was unanimous: Ashmedai, may his name be cursed,
was in the right. Nachman could only be saved if you, Dovid,
should renounce the contract you made with his henchman,
return the tainted wealth you received, and repent for your life of
wickedness. This repentance cannot be an idle gesture: You must
truly purge yourself of decades of accumulated sins. And you
must not create new sins in the process by wantonly harming
others. Nor can you exploit your penance to glorify yourself as
some type of suffering saint.

Dovid was dumbstruck, as he had never spoken of his affair
with Maryska, his fraudulent business dealings, or his promise to
Moshe. Even if Rachel had discerned some of these facts over the
years, she could not have known them all. Dovid confided in no
one but Moshe and even kept things from him. There is something
unusual about this visitor, Dovid concluded; he is no ordinary man.
Perhaps this is an emissary from the Throne of Glory.

Still, Dovid was affronted at the accusation he was a sinner or Moshe was a demon. He was a good man, he told himself, not always perfect, but then who is? And Moshe was no demon.

Dovid thus mounted his defense:

Old man, Eliyahu, whoever you are, you clearly know secrets I thought were hidden. But in the end you make no sense. I am no great sinner. I was an orphan, mistreated and persecuted, and a rich householder in this town took pity on me and employed me in his business. When I worked hard and proved my worth, he wed me to his daughter. As the sons of my father-in-law, may he rest in peace, showed no interest in the business, I inherited it. I owe my wealth to my hard work and talent and to nothing else.

Yes, fine, I cut a corner here and there, but who doesn't? The rich noblemen and the rich merchants always try to cheat me with false weights, with inferior merchandise, with any other clever scheme they can conjure up. I simply do what I must in the world. If I did not cheat them, they would just cheat me. Is that such a wonderful result? Is it a righteous deed to let yourself be fleeced?

The business with Maryska, I grant you that was a mistake. But it was brief, and it is hard on a man not to have his wife satisfy his needs. I did not create these needs of mine, and I do not want them. Why can't your friends hovering about the Throne of Glory relieve me of these desires?

I cannot let your slanders of Moshe go unanswered. A demon? He is no demon, he is a righteous man. Perhaps you are the demon—that might explain how you know so much. Moshe has always looked after Nachman's education, and pressed me to ensure the boy had only the best tutors. What kind of demon obsesses over the quality of a boy's education in the holy books?

I did not sell Nachman to Moshe. We made a match for Nachman to marry Moshe's daughter. What is wrong with that?

Moshe is a rich man, there will be an excellent dowry, and I trust Moshe to have raised a pious Jewish daughter.

So I think your talk, for all the secrets you somehow know, adds up to much slander and nonsense. Take your satchel and your cheese, and go harass the householders in some other town.

The old man shook his head sadly.

I cannot compel you. It is your choice to save your son or not. I have discharged my duty.

Dovid felt even angrier, rose, and intended to strike the insolent old beggar. But when Dovid stood and turned, he found himself a few steps from the door to his own house. Dovid was not sure how he had suddenly reached home or where the old man had gone, but with no target to strike, Dovid's rage dissolved and he yearned for sleep again.

Dovid walked inside. Standing in the front parlor, her hands twisted in knots, was Rachel in her nightgown. She was pacing back and forth. She looked eagerly at Dovid when he entered.

Dovid ignored her and walked past the parlor up the stairs. He wanted to rest, and to forget the old man. He did not want to talk to the mad harpy who had forced him to undergo this miserable exercise.

Rachel stood still and watched Dovid walk halfway up the stairs before she shook herself out of her trance and ran up after him. Rachel caught up with her husband at the top of the staircase.

She whispered:

Did you see him? Did he tell you how we can save Nachman?

Dovid ignored Rachel and lumbered towards his bed. It felt so good to close his eyes and lay down again on his back.

Rachel knelt by his bed and put her mouth to Dovid's ear: Please, you must tell me. I cannot sleep, I am terrified for my only son, my *Kaddish*.

More silence from Dovid.

Answer me, you must answer me.

Dovid finally mumbled a response:

I went to the *Bet Midrash*. I spoke to an old man, I assume he is the same old man. He said crazy things about Nachman and demons. He slandered me and Moshe. So I gave him a piece of my mind and came home. Now let me rest and quit with your nonsense.

Rachel was quiet for a few minutes, but she did not move away. Dovid, assuming she had gone to her bed, had let himself drift peacefully into heavy black sleep. But then Rachel's voice penetrated his slumber again:

He must have told you something about what to do. What did he tell you to do? Even if you won't do it, I will. What is wrong with you? Why won't you help our son?

Our son is fine. He is with Moshe and Moshe's family. He is probably too busy to write. Don't you think a young man thinks about things other than his silly mother?

Dovid pulled the blankets over his head and curled himself into a ball underneath them. He heard the sound of Rachel's faint footsteps walking away, followed by her muffled sobs. Dovid cursed her bitterly.

Over the next several days Dovid and Rachel avoided one another. There was no more sign of the old man. Indeed, when Dovid made discreet inquiries, he was told there had been no such traveler in the town. The beadle's insistence that no wandering old scholar had passed through soothed Dovid's nerves. He thought it all must have been a dream.

More days passed with no word from Nachman or Moshe. While Dovid told himself not to worry, the old man's words ate at him. He wished for a sign to disprove the old man's crazy talk: a letter from Moshe, perhaps, two or three sentences about how Nachman had impressed the town's scholars and was now learning the ins and outs of practical business, too. Or a request from Nachman to forward on some of his books, or maybe some of his clothes. The sign did not have to be dramatic, just enough to show Rachel—and his own waffling soul—that everything was all right. Right, Dovid thought, a small sign—is that too much to ask of the universe?

But nothing came. Dovid could not stop himself from feeling responsible for some terrible misfortune befalling Nachman, even though he told himself this was so much superstitious nonsense.

Dovid's temper became short. At the slightest pretext, he exploded in curses and reproaches at his employees, denouncing their incompetence and laziness and stupidity. He accused the household servants of stealing. When Hannah asked for money for a new dress, Dovid flew into a rage at her spendthrift habits and did not relent even when she ran away in tears.

And still there were no letters from Nachman or Moshe. Dovid wondered whether the old man had cast a spell to drive him insane. Dovid did not think the old man was really Eliyahu HaNavi or any other heavenly messenger, but the old man did know many of Dovid's secrets, so Dovid surmised the man must have been a sorcerer, probably hired by a business rival. He thought this silence from Nachman and Moshe was the sorcerer's trick.

Dovid decided to free himself from the malicious spell. He paid one of his agents to find and bring him a man well versed in the *kabbalah* who could lift curses. Two days later his agent returned with a short, smiling man with an unkempt red beard and rumpled clothes.

Dovid explained the situation, and offered a small fortune to the kabbalist to restore his sanity. The little man closed his eyes and rapidly mumbled various Hebrew and Aramaic incantations that made no sense to Dovid. Nevertheless Dovid was hopeful that whatever the little man was doing would end his suffering and he could soon resume normal life.

When the little man finished he opened his eyes and looked straight into Dovid. His expression was bitter. He extended a finger, almost in accusation, at Dovid.

Dovid forced an ingratiating smile and asked: What has been revealed to you? Can you help?

I cannot take your money, Reb Dovid. It is all spun by demons. You are in the demon's web, and I cannot help you. I have seen the heavenly decree, and I shudder for what will become of your ruined soul.

With that, the little man briskly walked away.

Dovid was more terrified than ever. Perhaps, he thought, the old man was Eliyahu HaNavi, and he had spoken the truth. He did seem to know so much …

Now came the terrible dreams. One night Nachman's flesh was being slowly burned away by smirking demons who laughed at his screams. Another night Dovid saw three beautiful women, tall and pale and blonde, kiss Nachman with black lips and caress him with forked serpent's tongues. Each place on his body touched by the lips and tongues turned to grey ash.

On a third night, Dovid dreamed he was dining with Moshe in a marble palace in a forest. Moshe sat at the head of the table; Dovid was at his left. The two were joking, like they used to joke with each other. In walked a tall stone gargoyle carrying a covered tray. Dovid froze in terror, but Moshe showed no surprise. The tray was placed in front of Moshe and the cover lifted. Sitting on the plate was Nachman's head severed from his body, but still alive. The head begged Moshe not to hurt it, but Moshe laughed and sank his fork into an eyeball.

And still there was no word from Nachman or Moshe. Dovid became convinced his wickedness had doomed his innocent and good son. Dovid decided he must try to save Nachman. No matter what the consequences, Dovid told himself, he must repent.

Yet Dovid hesitated. He enjoyed his large house and fine clothes and stuffed gullet. Did he really have to give this all up? What if, Dovid wondered, he made a public confession, ruined his fortune, and received a letter from Nachman a week later?

So Dovid vacillated between the urge to repent and the desire to keep his riches. He slept poorly, developing dark rings about his eyes. His mind could not focus clearly and he found himself unable to track the details of grain prices and shipments. His employees grew concerned and longed for the days when all they needed to worry about was Dovid's temper.

Dovid made his fateful choice one Saturday morning at the Great Synagogue. It was a grey day: cold, windy, with pounding rain. Dovid had been soaked on his way to pray and sat shivering in a corner. The weekly Torah portion was from the Book of Exodus and described how the Holy One, Blessed be He, punished the Egyptians for their hard-hearted wickedness with the slaughter of their first born sons.

Dovid saw the scene vividly: Pharaoh's little son, no more than eight years old, an innocent, gentle soul; in fact, the little boy loved to draw and paint. Dovid imagined the little Egyptian praying sweetly to his idols, he had no way to know they were false gods. And then the Angel of Death strode into the little boy's playroom and sliced his head off in one clean stroke to punish him for his father's sinful pride in refusing to free the Israelites from bondage.

Dovid wondered how Pharaoh could do something so cruel to his child. Were his crown and riches worth the death of a beautiful, innocent child? No—Pharaoh should have sacrificed it all, freely, willingly, eagerly, to save his son. That was what fathers did: They protected their children. Dovid saw the little Egyptian boy's eyes as the terrible sword was raised above his small head, and Dovid knew those panicked eyes were searching in vain for a father's protection.

Without fully realizing what he was doing, Dovid leaped to his feet and shouted at the man at the lectern chanting the weekly Torah portion:

Stop! Stop! You must be quiet, I must speak, I must confess, I must protect him.

Stop!

The Torah reader stopped and looked at Dovid. Baffled eyes in every direction turned to the wet, shivering, screaming man. Dovid strode up and addressed the Great Synagogue:

I must confess! I have done many wicked, forbidden acts. I fornicated with my maidservant, Maryska. I did this many times. My wealth has come to me through the use of false weights and measures, and I have defrauded many of you and other Jews and Polish lords. When the Holy *Shabbat* ends, I will write letters to everyone whom I have cheated and beg their forgiveness.

Dovid spoke these words in a mad headlong rush, barely pausing to breathe. He looked at no one in particular during his confession, but stared instead at a blank space in the wall between the men's section on the ground and the women's section in the balcony.

Once he had finished, Dovid walked briskly out of the sanctuary. He neither looked at anyone nor spoke to anyone, but strode back to his home and sat down in his kitchen. He poured a tall glass of brandy, half of which he downed in the first swig.

Dovid felt as if a twisting, tight grip on his limbs had now been released, and he experienced a sudden whirling lightness in his body. He was sure he had saved Nachman, or at least started to save him. He had faced up to his sins and he would repent; he was proud of his courage in doing so.

Dovid looked around his expensive house and laughed. Who needed any of this, he thought. I lived once as a poor beggar, performing the humble *mitzvoth*, good deeds, of reciting psalms for the sick and the dead. I committed no sins then, and followed the light of the Holy One, Blessed be He. It was only when I began to lust after riches that I fell into wickedness. I must cleanse myself of these false worldly idols and return to the path of righteousness, both for myself and for my Nachman. King Solomon was right: It is all empty vanity and there is nothing new under the sun.

Dovid reached over for his *tallit* (prayer shawl) bag, which he had put down on the kitchen table. He rummaged through it until he found an old, weather beaten book. It was no bigger than Dovid's palm and had a simple brown cover and brown back. There were no illustrations, and there was no commentary. It was a bare printing of the psalms. Dovid kissed the book's cover and caressed it. In his mind, he imagined the book as his true wife, an innocent, blushing Jewish maiden—Rebecca at the well—whom Dovid had abandoned and betrayed for worldly riches. But now Rebecca, in her simple white dress, standing in a simple white tent, in the Holy Land, saw her beloved returning to her.

Dovid finished the glass of brandy. He looked at the book of psalms and addressed it aloud: I am my beloved's and my beloved is mine. Dovid smiled again, and no longer wanted to be in his house. He took a loaf of black bread and some herring, and, together with his little brown book of psalms, walked to his grain silo at the edge of town.

The silo was empty as no business was conducted on the Holy *Shabbat*. Dovid sat in a corner near a window where the light was best. He ate his modest meal and spent the remainder of the *Shabbat* chanting psalms.

When evening came and the work week began again, Dovid walked over to his desk, lit a candle, and placed his account books and records to his right, and his small book of psalms to his left. In front of him were paper and ink. Dovid heaved a sigh, and commenced writing letters to each Jewish merchant and Polish lord he had defrauded. He consulted his account books to find the pertinent details for each victim. Dovid stayed up all through the night writing, not finishing until slightly past dawn. He placed the letters into a satchel he found nearby and he returned to reciting psalms.

Dovid's workers trickled in. They were stunned to see their employer madly swaying over some tiny book at his desk, with dark-ringed, bloodshot eyes. The workers did not look at Dovid or speak to him. Nor did they look at each other. They silently shuffled about the silo, each man trying to find a way to busy himself.

Dovid eventually looked up and surmised from the sun's angle in the sky that day had dawned. He closed his book, kissed it passionately, and put it in his pocket. Humming a melancholy *Shabbat* hymn, Dovid marched triumphantly out of the silo to deposit his many letters to be posted on Monday morning, after the Christians' Sabbath.

Dovid had no desire to return to his home or to his business. He imagined himself playing the part of the rich householder, merchant and father, and laughed so loudly that passersby stared. So, instead, Dovid walked and hummed along the town's main road in the direction opposite the grain silo until he had left town and come to a small grove of birch trees. He lay down on the grass between the trees and went to sleep in the moist dirt, like a traveling beggar. He felt a rush of happiness, and dreamed of his innocent maiden in the white tent. Nachman joined his father in the tent, and embraced him. Even the little eight-year-old Egyptian boy, Pharaoh's doomed son, joined them.

Rachel did not experience such peace. Rachel and Hannah had been sitting in the women's section of the Great Synagogue when they heard Dovid screaming in the sanctuary below. Rachel rushed to the curtain at the front of the women's section to hear better, but this proved unnecessary: Dovid's voice was clear throughout the whole balcony area where the women sat.

Rachel sat down after Dovid's speech. Her back was erect, and she stared at the curtain. No one in the women's section spoke. Rachel did not understand why he had done this. She did not yet feel anger or shame, but only bafflement. Had her Dovid gone crazy? she wondered. Maybe that was it—he had become insane. Perhaps, Rachel thought, the demons were coming after her, taking first her Nachman and now her Dovid's sanity.

Hannah crept over to her mother as the other women silently moved away. Hannah looked at her mother, but Rachel pretended not to notice. Hannah started to whisper something, but could not get any words out of her mouth.

The *rebbetzin* walked over to Rachel and said, softly, that Rachel appeared unwell and should probably go home to rest. Rachel quietly obeyed and went home, with Hannah at her side.

Dovid had already departed for the grain silo by the time Rachel and Hannah reached home. The two women entered the kitchen, where they saw a bottle of brandy and an empty glass. Rachel assumed that Dovid was home and would reappear shortly. She sat down at the table. Hannah sat down opposite. Neither spoke.

Shame washed over Rachel. How could she walk proudly around town, as the wife and daughter of well-respected Jewish householders, with everyone knowing her husband was an adulterer and a thief? What was to become of her and her girls now?

Hannah finally spoke up: Mother, I can't believe any of it is true. Father isn't like that. He is a good man, he is an honest man. Why would he say such things?

Rachel sighed at her daughter's words, but said nothing. Hannah said no more and soon left her mother alone. Rachel now seethed with rage. First Dovid had sold Nachman to demons, and now he had destroyed Rachel's life and no doubt her daughters' too. She cursed the day her father had brought him home. She rehearsed in her head the reproaches she would make to Dovid when he returned. She waited anxiously. Sure of the rightness of her cause, she was eager to sink her claws into his wicked hide.

But Dovid did not return. His workers came to the house and told Rachel he had not been seen since he went to post a thick packet of letters—had she seen Dovid? The workers were concerned; they were doing their best to keep the business running, but they needed Dovid's guidance. Rachel, however, could not help them.

The next wave of visitors was less friendly. Dovid's letters had been delivered, and a slew of lawsuits followed in their wake, both in Jewish and Gentile courts. Rachel was handed summons after summons for Dovid to appear at this proceeding or that one. Dovid, though, was nowhere to be found. Nevertheless, based on the admissions of guilt and detailed accounting in his letters, judgments were entered against Dovid across southern Poland.

Dovid's creditors swooped down to collect. His business assets were seized and auctioned off, and his workers lost their livelihoods and were forced to rely upon the community welfare funds. Several matches involving the children of these workers unraveled as the daughters could no longer offer the promised dowries. The shamed girls cried bitterly and cursed Dovid.

Dovid's business assets were not enough, however; his frauds had been so vast that his creditors could not satisfy their claims without seizing his household goods, too. Thus Dovid's—and Rachel's—house, furniture, linens, silverware, and even some clothes were auctioned away.

Rachel and her daughters were left destitute. Rachel wanted to divorce her husband and start a new life, but she could not. This was because her husband could not be found anywhere and she could not end the marriage unless he personally granted her a *'get,'* a bill of divorce. She was thus now an *agunah* under Jewish law, a woman chained to her marriage to an absent husband with no legal means of escape.

Rachel scrounged up what funds she could and hired a wagon to take her and her girls to the nearest one of her wealthy brothers. Her brother and sister-in-law greeted their surprise guests politely but coolly. With some difficulty, room was found in the house for the newcomers.

After the children had gone to sleep, Rachel spoke frankly to her brother and sister-in-law. They had, naturally, already heard of Dovid's mad confessions and sudden disappearance. Served Father right, her brother said, for marrying you off to a coarse ignoramus and then handing the business over to that stupid oaf.

Rachel forced herself not to cry. Don't speak of my Dovid, she said, he is gone. I am chained to him and impoverished, that is my punishment. But my girls did nothing wrong. What is to become of them? They need husbands—but how can they make a match with such shame and no dowries?

Her brother promised to help. It would not be easy. The girls would not get fine matches—no handsome scholars from wealthy and renowned families. But he believed he could raise large enough dowries to convince Jewish artisans to marry their sons to Rachel's daughters, despite the ugly shame of their father. However, he cautioned, first let the gossip die down a bit. Rachel gnawed on her lip at the thought of such low-born, unlearned grooms, but knew her brother was right.

Rachel's brother wrote to their other brothers, and Rachel's daughters were distributed among the different brothers' households. The girls were treated worse than relatives, but better than servants: They were forced to labor and clean alongside the domestic servants, but were still given decent clothes and ample food.

Hannah was the first to be married, in a match struck two years after Dovid's fall. The groom was the son and apprentice of a cobbler. The boy's family was initially repulsed at the thought of having such a wicked man's daughter as a bride, but, as Rachel's brother predicted, changed their minds when they saw the generous dowry.

Hannah's uncle also paid for a fine dress and wedding celebration. Rachel rejoiced at Hannah's wedding and thought her daughter was the most beautiful of brides. There was no shame in marrying a cobbler, she told herself. He made an honest living and would earn enough to feed and clothe his family. But part of her still felt a tinge of shame when the cobbler groom, who could barely read any Hebrew, did not even attempt to deliver a learned discourse to his guests, as a more scholarly groom would have done. Still, she had lived to see her daughter under the *chuppah*, and that was a blessing.

Rachel saw her other daughters married in the succeeding years. The stigma of Dovid's shame slowly faded, and Rachel and her brothers were able to secure a better class of bridegroom— from artisans to small merchants and shopkeepers. While still no scholars or wealthy men, Rachel's sons-in-law were honest Jews who made decent livings. She was comforted by the thought that no one would starve.

As memories dimmed and Rachel's daughters moved to distant towns, Rachel was in the happy position of being questioned by new acquaintances about her husband's fate and how she had become an abandoned wife, an *agunah*. Rachel felt giddy as she heard these always embarrassed inquiries: Pardon me for asking, I know it is none of my business, but a person cannot help but wonder how you were left in such a state?

Rachel would start to grin at the thought that her new friend was ignorant of Dovid's shame. Knowing this was the wrong reaction, she would force herself into an anguished grimace and stare at the ground.

This pose would yield further rushes of embarrassed words: Oh no, I am sorry, forgive me, I don't mean to pry …

Rachel would look up and sigh. With theatrically sad eyes, Rachel would tell her preferred version of the story:

No, it is all right. It has been many years since my husband left. He was a merchant. One day, he told me he needed to go to the fair in Leipzig. He had gone many times before, so who would think anything of it? He hired a wagon, packed his things, and was off. I thought nothing was unusual until two weeks had gone by with no word. Usually by then he had at least sent me a letter. Sometimes he had already made it back home. But this time, nothing. Another week goes by and still nothing.

So I went to my friend Beyle and asked if she had heard from her husband, who had gone to the same fair. Of course, she said, he is sitting in the next room smoking a pipe. So I went to the next room and I said, Reb Itzik, do you know where my husband is? He said, how should I know? So I said, but wasn't he with you at the fair?

And now Itzik puts down his pipe and gives me this strange look, like I just told him I had given birth to a chicken. Itzik said: He wasn't at the fair. Come to think of it, he usually is at the fair, but not this year.

Now I started to panic. I had, after all, these young girls to look after, and they needed a father to support them. So I ran about town seeking news, but no one knew anything. I sent letters flying in every direction, but still no one knew where he was.

You can guess who showed up pretty soon at my doorstep: creditors. Right before that husband of mine had disappeared he seemed to have borrowed money from everyone in Poland. I did not realize one man could sign so many promissory notes. So the vultures did what they always do, and gone were my home, furniture, linen, even some of my clothes.

By the mercy of the Holy One, Blessed be He, I was taken in by my brothers who arranged the girls' dowries, and I have had the good luck to live to see each of my girls under the *chuppah*. But as for me, I am stuck as an *agunah*, and I will never be able to marry again.

At this point, a tear would drift down her cheek and Rachel would sigh again.

Rachel repeated this tale so often that it circulated more widely than the true recollections of Dovid's spectacular confession. Soon anyone offering the details of the true course of events was denounced for slandering the good name of the long-suffering *agunah*. Rachel herself was no longer sure where to draw the line between memory and invention. Nor did she care.

Rachel did not feel sorrow at being an *agunah*. True, at first her anguish was real. She had wanted to remarry, preferably a wealthy man with a more stable personality and greater learning than her Dovid; she felt bitter at her trapped state. In time, however, she was happy not to marry. Once her children had married she realized there were neither fathers nor husbands to curb her actions, nor any maternal responsibilities to weigh her down. She was in control of her days and pointed to her *agunah* status as the unfortunate reason she could not entertain any offers to remarry.

Rachel spent her time traveling among her daughters' and brothers' households. She enjoyed being in motion and exulted in meeting new people and seeing new towns. She burst with a restless energy. Being a chained woman had set her free.

Yet there was one nagging source of pain: Nachman, her beautiful son Nachman, her *Kaddish*. After Dovid's disappearance she prayed desperately for Eliyahu to return and to help her save Nachman. She was certain she had somehow failed to do what should have been done to save him and that she was to blame for his suffering. Rachel would try to block him out of her mind, but suddenly, at some unpredictable hour, she would hear his soft voice chanting from the Talmud, slightly muffled, the way she had heard him as a boy studying in the library in her house. The sound of these soft chants forced Rachel to sob loudly and uncontrollably.

Sometimes one of her daughters would try to comfort Rachel. This infuriated her. She would either ignore the girl or, if that did not work, smack the child hard across her face. Rachel knew this was wrong, would feel horrible afterwards, and would cover the child's welts with kisses and hot tears of guilty love. But she found her emotions hard to control.

Rachel's daughters learned not to speak of their absent brother and did not tell their husbands or children they ever had a brother, Nachman. Terrified of their mother's flying sharp claws, the girls erased Nachman from their memories and their family stories. As the years went by, Rachel, too, forgot Nachman. She tried so hard not to think about him anymore, not to worry about him, that he became a ghost and then a shadow, and then he was gone.

Still, with no Nachman, Rachel became obsessed with having a grandson. She had only daughters, she would lament, and girls cannot recite *Kaddish* for the souls of their departed parents. Rachel was scared she would die and, without the protection of a male child saying *Kaddish* for her, she would be hounded in her grave by demons.

Rachel saw her fate in her dreams: She saw herself dead, inert, with her daughters weeping over her body, then her daughters weeping as she went into the grave. Underground, in the cold, damp darkness of the earth, Rachel would start to hear cackling and laughing. A hand—red, scaly, and burning hot—would grab her, then another, and another, and she would writhe in pain from the burning heat and the sharp, piercing scales. The demons would fling her soul high into the night sky where they would chase her and mock her and beat her with iron rods. Rachel would beg for mercy. But the demons would taunt her: There is no one to say *Kaddish* for you, we can play with your soul to our delight, you will never make it to Paradise. Sometimes she would look into a demon's face and see Nachman staring back at her.

Rachel was thus understandably excited when Hannah became pregnant for the first time. She convinced herself the child would be a boy, who would grow up to say *Kaddish* for his grandmother's soul. She saw signs everywhere: Hannah's belly swelled large, which must mean a boy; the baby kicked constantly, which also must mean a boy—girls were lazy, but boys were active. Hannah craved goose fat, and only a boy could demand so much animal fat for big, boyish bones.

In her dreams Rachel now taunted the demons with the fact that she would soon have a grandson, whose sweet chanting of the *Kaddish* for her soul would turn their iron rods to dust and open a flower-strewn path to Paradise. The dream demons fled in terror.

Hannah's labor came. After a long night of screaming and pushing, the midwife announced that Hannah had given birth to a beautiful baby girl. Hannah dictated a letter to her mother, who was staying with one of Hannah's sisters in a different town. The letter was joyous and filled with thanks to the Holy One, Blessed be He.

Rachel read the letter from Hannah and shed angry tears. How could Hannah do this to me? she thought. That was supposed to be a boy. Rachel read the letter over repeatedly, with the strange hope she had misread its contents. But the words refused to cooperate. Rachel felt the words were spiting her, taunting her with their sarcastic joy in announcing that Rachel still had no one to say *Kaddish* for her soul.

Two years later Hannah was again in labor. Rachel did not trust her daughter anymore to produce the needed little boy, and, even though she was in the same town as Hannah at that time, Rachel only tardily and reluctantly went to her daughter's room to assist the midwife. But this time the Holy One, Blessed be He, smiled upon Rachel: Hannah gave birth to her grandson. Rachel had a *Kaddish*, and the demons would never get their hands on her.

Rachel beamed with joy on the day of her grandson's *Brit Milah*, the circumcision ceremony. She ate slice after slice of honey cake and could not stop praising the eight-day-old child: how handsome he was already, with a precocious mound of thick black hair; how his gaze at the world showed a secret wisdom he could not yet express. This child would do wondrous things, she was sure of it. The other guests at the ceremony smiled politely as Rachel went on, and looked for an excuse to drift towards more interesting company. But Rachel did not care. Nothing mattered except the fact that she had a boy, beautiful and wise she was sure, to say *Kaddish* for her when the time should come.

It was now the point in the ceremony when the child's name would be announced for the first time. The father said that Hannah had insisted on a particular name in honor of her deceased great uncle, may he rest in peace: Nachman.

Rachel felt the joy inside her dissolve; she stumbled slightly, and grabbed the back of a chair to support herself. How could Hannah? she seethed to herself.

Rachel concentrated hard and controlled herself. The fate of the real Nachman was a tightly held secret, so there was no point in exposing Rachel's sorrow and shame to everyone. Let them think this is in honor of Great Uncle Nachman, whomever he may be in Hannah's imagination.

Later that night Rachel lay down in her bed in the town's inn. It was dark and quiet, but she could not sleep. Rachel stared at the ceiling, with eyes wide open, and muttered to herself, over and over again, the name Nachman. She saw the infant boy's pudgy face in her mind.

She tried to imagine the other Nachman, her Nachman, but the images blurred. She saw the outline of his body as a small boy, but his face blurred when Rachel tried to focus upon it. She could still hear her Nachman chanting sweetly from the Talmud, but the sound had grown faint in her memory, and she struggled to hear it.

Rachel reflected: She never did actually learn the ultimate fate of her Nachman. No doubt he came to a bad end in the clutches of that vile demon calling himself Moshe, may he be cursed. Rachel imagined Nachman felled with a blow from a demon's iron rod, crying for his mother with his last breath.

Rachel imagined how Nachman's holy soul must have been greeted in the world to come. No doubt the Holy One, Blessed be He, had plans for this soul and had expected him to fulfill some glorious task. The Holy One, Blessed be He, had even sent Eliyahu HaNavi himself down to the lower world to intervene and save Nachman from Dovid's folly in handing the boy over to demons. And then Dovid botched it all up again and did not do whatever was necessary to save Nachman. Thus, Nachman's soul was an unexpected early arrival in Paradise.

Rachel imagined the angels clustered around the Throne of Glory debating what to do about this calamity. There may even have been an alarm that Ashmedai, king of the demons, had pulled off such a coup as to ensnare and murder one of the holy saints who were needed so desperately in the mortal world. Finally, a decision was reached: Nachman's soul would be sent down, back to Earth, into a new body.

Rachel smiled at the darkness in her room. Her new Nachman was her old Nachman: Her son's soul was reborn in the body of her infant grandson. Rachel felt a current of warm energy course through her. She was sure now she had been reunited with her Nachman, and he would say *Kaddish* for her soul. She whispered a prayer of thanks to the Holy One, Blessed be He, and promised to do a better job protecting this gentle, saintly soul.

Rachel felt light as a feather, and as she drifted into slumber, she felt herself float into the arms of smiling angels.

VII. The Hidden Saint and the Severed Head

WORD SPREAD AMONG the Jews of White Russia and even some of the more superstitious gentiles: A *lamed-vovnik*, one of the thirty-six hidden saints for whose sake the Holy One, Blessed be He, will never bring another flood to destroy the world, was roaming the countryside. As befits a *lamed-vovnik*, the man was a humble beggar. His clothes were wrinkled, ripped, and stained, although they oddly still bore a trace, here and there, of having once been expensive, fashionable garments. The man traveled with only one possession, a small book of psalms, which he referred to as his *bashert*, his true love and destined match. The *lamed-vovnik* claimed to have no learning apart from his psalms.

Despite his poverty and ignorance, the *lamed-vovnik* was forever doing good deeds. Wherever he went he would read psalms day and night for the sick and the dead, asking only for a crust of black bread and a drop of schnapps to keep body and soul together. He would pray fervently until eventually his exhausted limbs could not be pushed any longer, and then he would lie down on a bench or a floor of a synagogue, or *Bet Midrash*, or poor house to sleep, cradling and caressing his little book of psalms, sometimes even kissing it. I am yours and you are mine, he would whisper to the book.

The *lamed-vovnik* secretly performed other righteous deeds. For example, if he could lay his hands on a small axe, he would wander, alone, deep into a nearby forest and cut logs of firewood. Then the *lamed-vovnik*, doing his best to avoid being seen, would deliver this free firewood to poor households in the towns and villages. Many an ageing widow in the small Jewish towns of White Russia gave prayers of gratitude because, by a miracle, precious firewood had appeared, which she could not have afforded to buy, but was much needed to survive the brutal winter.

The *lamed-vovnik* was sometimes asked about his past. He was an orphan, he said, his parents had died at the hands of Chmielnicki's murderers when he was a small boy, and he was raised by relatives who could barely afford to feed him. Once grown, he had taken to a life of begging and wandering with his book of psalms. Had he ever had a wife and children? No, he would respond, he was a poor beggar who lacked the means to support a family. He was content if he had a hunk of black bread and a place to lay his head down at night.

One day the *lamed-vovnik* was wandering on a forest road as night fell. He felt a drop of rain hit his nose and saw dark storm clouds above. Looking for shelter, the *lamed-vovnik* spied a building to the side of the road.

The building turned out to be an abandoned ruin. He surmised it was an old fort, as there was a small watchtower and a corner of the courtyard where rusted, broken guns lay in a heap. The *lamed-vovnik* sat down in a corner where he judged the roof to be still secure and tried to sleep, although the sound of the thunder kept waking him.

As his eyes became accustomed to the dark, the *lamed-vovnik* saw an altar of sorts standing in the opposite corner of the room.

To his surprise, there were no crosses or other Christian symbols, but rather a small wooden statue of a man with long hair and a long beard holding an axe in one hand and a lightning bolt in the other. The statue was riding a chariot, also carved from the same wood, which two wooden goats pulled. While the rest of the abandoned ruin was cracked and decayed, this idol appeared to have been carved just that day and had not a blemish.

The *lamed-vovnik* thought he saw the statue of the forest god look at him and smirk. This is an idol, a false god, the *lamed-vovnik* told himself, it is as dead as any broken off branch. But he could not shake the terrible feeling that the idol was watching him and laughing at him. As the rain pounded harder and the thunder came closer, the wooden god's laugh seemed to grow louder. The *lamed-vovnik* tried to distract himself by reciting psalms, but the words stuck in his throat. He felt his heart palpitating. That wicked laugh was suffocating him.

In this terrified state the *lamed-vovnik* suddenly heard, through the thunder, rain, and evil laughter, a soft singing. The voice was female and quite beautiful. The *lamed-vovnik* did not recognize the song; the tune did not sound Jewish to his ears.

The strange, lovely music was coming from the direction of a window halfway between his corner and the menacing idol. The *lamed-vovnik* looked outside through the window, but saw no signs of rain or lightning, even though he could still hear the storm clearly behind him. There was only the singing, a quiet night, and a tall, round, stone tower. Eager to get away from the storm and the idol, the *lamed-vovnik* crawled through the window into the calm clearing.

The storm vanished and so did the fort. The *lamed-vovnik* was amazed by this marvel and thought he must be under the protection of the Holy One, Blessed be He. The *lamed-vovnik* recalled the wondrous tales he had heard of Jews waylaid in the forest during the holy *Shabbat* who had entered magical dwellings where they shared the holiday with Abraham, Isaac, and Jacob, and ate the cooking of Mother Rachel.

The *lamed-vovnik* walked to the door of the tower, which was slightly ajar. The music grew louder and clearer as he approached. The *lamed-vovnik* walked inside.

Past the vestibule there was a winding stone staircase lit with candles placed carefully in notches on the walls. There was no sign of any other person except for the sound of the lovely singing, which grew closer still as the *lamed-vovnik* ascended the stairs. He walked up for some time. When his tired bones reached the top of the staircase, there was finally a small landing at the end of which was a stone door.

The *lamed-vovnik* pushed the door open and entered a large room illuminated by a massive chandelier jammed with candles. Despite its size, the chandelier gave off a light that was dim and somehow made the room seem pale. On the walls were book-shelves, with more books than the *lamed-vovnik* knew existed.

The singing had stopped, and the sudden silence frightened the *lamed-vovnik*. He reached into his pocket for his book of psalms to recite a prayer to the Holy One, Blessed be He. When he opened his book, however, he saw that the name of the Holy One, Blessed be He, was blacked out on the page. The *lamed-vovnik* quickly thumbed through several more pages, and each was the same: The name of the Holy One, Blessed be He, was blacked out. The *lamed-vovnik* did not understand how this could happen and in a panic tried to recite a psalm from memory, but the words some-how failed him. He stumbled each time when he came to the name of the Holy One, Blessed be He.

Then the *lamed-vovnik* heard a voice, hollow and low, and somehow familiar:

His name is not welcome here.

The *lamed-vovnik's* eyes searched wildly for someone in the room, but he saw no one. He did now notice, however, that there was a rectangular table in the middle of the room, on which the bust of a human head was mounted on a flat silver base. This head was remarkably lifelike and appeared to be the face of someone the *lamed-vovnik* knew, but could not place.

The *lamed-vovnik* approached the head. He thought it was looking at him. He reached out and touched the bust's forehead, which felt like real skin. There was even fresh sweat.

Please do not touch me, Father.

The *lamed-vovnik* stepped back. The head was alive and speaking to him.

What are you? Why do you call me Father?

Father, it is me, Nachman, your child. You have finally come to visit me.

This cannot be. You were supposed to be saved. I gave up everything I received from Moshe. I repented so you would be saved. How can this be you? I did everything to save you.

The demons upheld their end of the bargain and you upheld yours. What you did with your payment was not their concern. The demon you call Moshe brought me to this place many years ago and sliced my head off. He then recited an incantation, a demon rite, and placed my head upon this table. I can speak and reason, and it is my job to prophesy for the demons. They needed a soul purified by years of study of the Torah to have the ability to see things hidden from them.

But this can't be. How can I save you? I spoke to Eliyahu HaNavi, and he promised that my repentance would save you. I gave away everything for you. Please, tell me.

I speak truth only to demon-kind. To you, I am a deceiver. My words to you are: Your soul is so black that you cannot discern truth from falsehood.

But can't I save you? Is your body here somewhere—can you be reattached?

The head ceased to speak. Its eyes glassed over and became somehow vacant.

The *lamed-vovnik* sat down facing the severed head. He looked at it for a long time and cried. In his heart he begged the Holy One, Blessed be He, to forgive him and to safeguard Nachman's soul. The *lamed-vovnik* reached out to stroke the head's cheek. His hand burned at the touch, and he had to pull it back.

The singing started again, beautiful, soft, and female. Although the tune was again unfamiliar to the *lamed-vovnik*, he was somehow drawn to it. He thought the music was coming from outside. Unable to bear the vacant look in Nachman's eyes, the *lamed-vovnik* left the library room and walked quickly back down the stone staircase. Once outside, the *lamed-vovnik* saw a woman singing under a tree. As the music made him feel safe, he walked towards her.

The tree was tall and broad. Halfway up its old, monstrously large trunk, was a carved face of a bearded god with long hair—the face of the idol from the ruin. But the *lamed-vovnik* did not notice the old god's face watching him this time, so entranced was he by the woman's song.

The *lamed-vovnik* walked calmly to her. She was naked, with long blonde hair. She put her arms around his neck and smiled into his eyes.

Maryska? the *lamed-vovnik* whispered. Is that you, Maryska?

The woman said nothing. She pressed her lips to his, and reached her tongue into his mouth. Even though she could not still be singing, the sound of her song continued to echo in the *lamed-vovnik's* ears, and he felt that he and Maryska were floating together on a cloud.

The woman's tongue stretched to the back of the *lamed-vovnik's* mouth, and then down his throat where it coiled itself tightly.

The *lamed-vovnik* could not breathe. He tried to break free of the woman's kiss, but to no avail.

Dovid's dead body lay in the forest, neglected, for many years. It eventually decomposed and was absorbed into the soil as food for the tree with the malevolent forest idol's bearded face.

There was no *Kaddish* said for Dovid's soul.

www.ingramcontent.com/pod-product-compliance
Lightning Source LLC
Chambersburg PA
CBHW032017180726
48283CB00008B/2721